Monsters In The Moonlight
Creepy Short Stories

Marcus Starr

Manor House

Library and Archives Canada
Cataloguing in Publication

Title: Monsters in the Moonlight: Creepy Short Stories /
/ Marcus Starr
Names: Starr, Marcus, author.
Identifiers: Canadiana 2023057484X |
ISBN 9781998938094 (hardcover) |
ISBN 9781998938087 (softcover)
Subjects: LCGFT: Horror fiction. | LCGFT: Short stories.
Classification: LCC PS8637.T375 M66 2023 |
DDC C813/.6—dc23

Note: This novel is a work of fiction. Any resemblance to locations or persons alive or dead is purely coincidental.

Cover art: Romolo Tavani/ Shutterstock / (Picture: Zombie Hand Rising Out of a Grave).

First Edition
Cover Design-layout / Interior- layout: Michael Davie
206 pages / approx. 60,000 words.   All rights reserved.
Published 2023   / Copyright 2023
Manor House Publishing Inc.
452 Cottingham Crescent, Ancaster, ON, L9G 3V6
www.manor-house-publishing.com   (905) 648-4797

*"From the critically acclaimed, award-winning author of **Nora's Curse** comes **Monsters in the Moonlight**, an outstanding collection of superb horror stories – a truly gripping must-read..."*
- **Michael B. Davie**, author, *The Late Man*

This project has been made possible [in part] by the Government of Canada. **« Ce projet a été rendu possible [en partie] grâce au gouvernement du Canada.**

For my Mother

Table of Contents:

Cabin Fever

My goal was to record a solo album at the cabin by the lake. I'm certainly not the first musician to do this. Google 'Cabin Fever' and see for yourself.

The cabin was built by my great-grandfather, and has remained in the family ever since. Naturally, it's been spruced up over the years; it now has running water, a high-powered generator for electricity, plus an indoor toilet, a recent addition, after a bat got tangled in my ex-wife's hair while she was having a tinkle.

Which leads me to why I came out here in the first place, in the middle of Nowheresville Ontario, in the cold of the early Spring. My marriage ended two weeks before Christmas. My wife dumped me, then she made off with her younger and more handsome co-worker Carl. I hate Carl, but I digress. Needless to say, I was at a crossroads.

I started writing songs.

It was slow going at first, but once I scratched out the first couple songs, the floodgates opened and the rest followed accordingly. By Spring, I'd composed enough songs for a solo acoustic album.

I brought two acoustic guitars: my Gibson J-100 and a vintage Harmony, circa 1960, which I used for open-tuning and slide guitar. I also brought some hand drums and shakers, a plethora of high-quality microphones and my laptop; plus, a bottle of single malt scotch and plenty of grub.

It's a three-and-a-half-hour drive, straight north. The cabin is so far off the beaten path that not even Google knows of its existence. I've done this drive more times than I can count, but it's never easy. I even got lost on my way up, and not for the first time. Eventually, after doubling back, I found the correct side road, and made it just before sunset. Not a good way to start.

The cabin was eerily quiet. Darkness was impending, so I quickly got to work. First, I lit the kerosene lanterns, then I started the generator and checked to see if the toilet was working. It was. There was enough chopped wood and kindling to last all week, if needed. I fired up the wood stove. The cabin warmed up wonderfully. Then I unloaded my gear and put the food away.

Finally, I could relax. I sighed as my buttocks hit the familiar feel of the old Chesterfield. A lifetime of memories surrounded me: Mom's rocking chair cradled in the corner; Dad's Remington hanging dutifully on the adjacent wall, next to the mounted antlers; the collection of family photos on the mantelpiece, including a picture of me with my beloved grandmother, taken at this very cabin, and a wedding photo of my ex-wife in her stunning gown, somewhere off the coast of St. Lucia. I rested my feet on the coffee table and sipped my drink, trying not to tear up.

Unfortunately, my mind scurried down the wrong rabbit hole, and I was lured into a deep depression. My life was in shambles. This was Rock Bottom. Filled with grief, I found solstice in the bottle, until sleep took me under its spell.

Day One:

I awoke to strange noises.

Scrape. Scrape. Scrape.

"What the heck is that?"

I rubbed my eyes. My mouth was as dry as a musician's sense of humour. My head hurt. I needed water and Tylenol, pronto.

"I'm too old for this," I reminded myself. "No more booze," I promised. "I have a record to record."

I made a hearty breakfast of bacon and eggs and strong coffee. I ate ravenously. All the while, the scraping noises continued. They were coming from the lake. This cabin is built on a peninsula. It's completely surrounded by water and tall trees. This type of solitude can induce claustrophobia and/or agoraphobia in certain individuals. This cabin certainly has a dark history in that regard. My grandmother, also a musician, committed suicide here back in the eighties. It was tragic.

Scrape. Scrape. Scrape.

"I should check that out," I grumbled, while groping my coffee mug. "Better grab the gun on the way out. Just in case."

As always, the view was stunning. The soft morning sun sparkled over the tops of trees, which provided plenty of shade in the afternoon. The deck is cozy, with enough room to sit and read a paperback, while enjoying the generous backdrop. Beyond the deck lurks McNamee Lake.

With squinted eyes I scanned the ashen lake. Aside from the blustering breeze sweeping up pieces of icy snow and the gaggle of Canadian geese bobbing about their business, the lake was deserted.

Scrape. Scrape. Scrape.

The sound sent chills down my spine, as if warning me not to stick around for the week. When I retreated to the safety of the cabin, the sound followed me.

Scrape. Scrape. Scrape.

Then it hit me: The lake ice was rubbing against itself. It's thawing. This is normal. Lakes do that this time of year. This should be obvious. I shrugged my paranoia off as jitters. I was in solitude, with no internet, surrounded by a lake that's making strange noises. Plus, I was grieving. I'll get over it. Time to get to work.

Having set up shop in the living room, I placed a microphone in close proximity to my guitar, and three more in various spots around the cabin, including one strategically placed on the ceiling, hoping to capture the full spectrum of sound. I placed the vocal mic in front of me and tuned the guitars. Ready to roll.

With the instruments and recording equipment in check, I went about setting up the cameras. My iPhone provided a close-up of my guitar work, while my GoPro captured the full performance as well as the ambience of the rustic cottage.

At first, my fingers were clumsy, my voice lacking confidence. I couldn't find my groove. It's not every day one finds themselves alone, in a hundred-year-old log cabin, encapsulated by a creaky lake. My voice and my fingers needed time to warm up. By the third cup of coffee, things started to improve. It was tiresome, but by the end of the day I managed to record three songs: Hard Luck & Trouble, Country Livin', Whiskey Drinkin', and a spiteful little number called So Long to Know You.

Nightfall fell fast. After enjoying a steak dinner and some Scotch, I retired to the couch. So far, so good.

Day Two:

I awoke with a terrible sweat, shaking. Nightmares dissolved into my mind like ice cubes slipping into a cool drink on a warm day. I forced myself out of bed, urinated, then went straight for the coffee maker.

Coffee in hand, I meandered to the deck, ready to relax and have a cup. However, before I could nestle into the lawn chair, something weird happened: a brisk breeze brushed the back of my neck, sending a searing shot coursing through my body, spilling my coffee in the process.

"What the…"

Something whizzed past me.

I wasn't alone.

I went for my gun, and didn't doddle. Then I searched the premises, gun in hand, looking for intruders. It's a small plot of land. It didn't take long. The snow on the ground had recently melted. In its place came a mixture of cranky mud and slippery slosh. Chomping along the cold, sodden soil made me miserable. My feet and socks were soaked.

Then I noticed the tracks.

The tracks were unlike any I'd seen: long curvy claws at the tip, cut deep and wide; bear-like, except twice as large and spaced further apart. Judging from the depth of them, the thing was gargantuan. I scratched my head. Something about the track marks seemed wrong. I returned to the cabin and fetched my phone. I wanted to document them, so when I'm back on Wi-Fi, I can search them up.

The problem was, when I returned, the tracks were gone. I was bewildered. This was a different version of outside. Moments ago, the morning was full of birdsong. Not anymore. I rubbed my eyes in disbelief.

"I gotta get out of here," I said, not trusting the sound of my voice.

"Don't be ridiculous," I answered. "I just got here."

I was right. I marched back inside the cabin and put the shotgun back in its rightful spot on the wall. I poured myself a fresh cup and drank my coffee in quiet desperation. Something wasn't right. The air in the cabin was too thick. The silence was deafening. I'd nearly forgotten my true purpose for coming here. My eyes glanced at the old Remington, next to the antlers, and remained there for an uncomfortable length of time.

Too weary to eat, I unlatched my acoustic guitar case and pulled out my Gibson, placing it neatly on the stand. When I opened the other case, it was empty. I panicked. That old Harmony was irreplaceable. I ran outside, gun in hand, murder in mind. But of course, nothing was out there.

I scurried into the cabin, ready to give up and go home. To my surprise, my old Harmony was sitting on the stand, next to the Gibson, gleaming. Impossible. Had it always been there? I shrugged. With shaky hands, I strummed a chord. It was in tune.

Reluctantly, I fired up the laptop and went to work. The first song I recorded was a delta blues number called Hammer Song, both a tribute to 'Hammer Town' Ontario, as well as a nod to American folk legend, John Henry. The song came out swimmingly.

I tried my hand at it again, but nothing beat that first take. The blues licks were ferocious, the vocals drenched in gut-retching soul. I was pleased. And hungry. I plundered through some bacon and eggs, then I made a rough mix of the song. It needed something special, so I added some shakers and a djembe for support.

That's when I noticed the applause.

At first, I thought it was the percussion, but upon further review, it was more than that. Underneath my voice and guitar was an actual audience. For real. They were clapping along, cheering sporadically, even catcalling from time to time. I pulled up the files from the laptop, looking for visual clues as to where the sound was coming from, but found none. Instead, my laptop slammed shut. I leapt out of the chair, screaming in surprise.

"Who's in here?" I demanded. "Show yourself."

Someone was in the cabin. It was undeniable at this point.

"Do you want me to leave?"

I regretted asking this. Truth be told, I wanted to stay. I had work to do, not to mention my Grand Finale. I closed my eyes and took a deep breath; my eyes sprung open, then I grabbed my Gibson and strummed an open G chord. It sounded like an ocean. I restarted my computer, pressed record, then began picking through a tune called Sorry Again, a sappy fingerstyle song I wrote shortly after my marriage ended. Again, I nailed it on the first take.

As I finished the final chord, I was surprised to see the glow of the setting sun peaking through the adjacent window. I checked the time: 7:51pm.

"That can't be right," I told myself.

But it was. Apparently, time was not on my side. The day was spent in hours, but the music was effortless. After blending the guitar with the vocals, I pressed play, and was immediately awestruck. My voice was divine, my guitar an orchestra.

That said, I didn't know what to make of the voices. With the volume turned up on the headphones, you could hear them chattering amongst themselves at the quiet parts, singing along to their favourite parts. Judging from the recording, you'd think I was performing to a live audience.

"At least they're applauding," I said in a wobbly voice. "I'd hate to see what would happen if they were displeased."

By now it was pushing eleven, as ludicrous as that was. I made some canned ravioli and washed it down with single malt scotch. Just a little, I reminded myself. No more hangovers. I added another log to the fire, then I curled up on the Chesterfield and slipped into a deep and troublesome sleep.

Day Three:

Something startled me awake. I'd been having a nightmare. In it, I was being chased through the woods by a grisly monster. Bizarrely, the monster was singing, but I didn't recognize the song, nor did I understand the words. Those sinister-sounding syllables lingered, as I stooped over the couch, scared shitless, unsure if I could go through with this.

After emptying my bladder, I grabbed the gun and grumbled outside. The air was basement-damp, and chilled me to the bone. A copse of soggy Black Spruces bordered the semi-frozen lake, the leaves ridding themselves of last night's rainfall. To my horror, those inhuman claw marks emerged from the lake, making great strides, leading to the back of the cabin. I cocked the gun, then sprinted around to the deck, fully expecting a confrontation. The deck was empty, save for a paperback resting on a crooked lawn chair with coffee stains dripping down its side. The lake cranked out a creepy sound, startling me. Then something nuzzled the nape of my neck.

"I gotta get outta here," I snapped.

I rushed inside and began the daunting task of packing up. Yet, as I was putting my guitars away, something prevented me from doing so. I just couldn't bring myself to leave. Instead, I relistened to the work I'd done on Day One. The songs were extraordinary. That said, the auspicious audience was impossible to ignore.

I was furious. Someone or something was hijacking the mixes. My mind jumped to many conclusions, each scarier than the last. Ultimately, I shrugged it off. What choice did I have? I tuned up the old Harmony, and cut the sixth song: a blues number using DADGAD tuning, called Fell in Mud. This was my most difficult song to play. Originally, my plan was to record the guitar first, then overdub the vocals afterwards. But I decided against it. Instead, I recorded it in one take.

"Unbelievable."

I was stunned by my performance. My voice was gnarly, full of emotion, my fingerpicking precise and with purpose. The unseeing audience filled in the quiet bits. The idea that I wasn't alone was indeed freaking me out, but the results spoke for themselves. So, with butterflies swirling in the pit of my stomach, I reached for my Gibson, flat pick in hand, looking to keep the momentum going. I tuned up, then pressed record.

I strummed a G7sus chord, letting it sustain. Then, as I leaned into the opening riff of The Devil I Know, someone – or something – spoke my name. I jumped out of my seat in surprise. Then my blood went cold. I hate being interrupted.

"Who's there?" I spat.

My voice fell to the floor with a thud. No answer came. I knew it wasn't safe here, alone in the cabin, but the allure of my tobacco-burst Gibson guitar was irresistible. I sat back down, took a deep breath, and hit record.

Sure enough, just as I started the riff, a voice spoke inside my headphones. This time, I kept playing. Although my hands were shaky, I managed to complete the song. It wasn't perfect, so I did another take. Then another. With each take, I was bombarded with bellows and hollers from the omnipresent audience. It was arduous. But after nine tries, I finally got it.

Wearily, I mixed the vocals with the blended guitars until I produced a pleasing sound. Upon playback, those spectators were as pesky as ever.

"I'll have to fix that when I get home," I said, stone-cold terrified.

Having eaten dinner and tidied up, I loaded some wood into the stove before collapsing onto the couch. I was spent. Darkness engulfed me. The walls were closing in, the air difficult to breathe. Panic turned to despair. Would anyone notice if I disappeared? Would anyone care? No. I was insignificant. The world would go on without me, as if I'd never existed. The wretchedness of my personal life came flooding back. All the while, my eyes fixated on the shotgun on the wall.

"You came here to kill yourself," I reminded myself.

I nodded. My plan was to go out with a bang. I'll make my final record – a masterpiece that the world would remember me by – then I'll place the barrel of the shotgun into my mouth, and blow my brains to smithereens, Cobain style.

"You're not gonna chicken out, are you?" I asked.

I shook my head.

"Good. Stick to the plan."

Footsteps startled me; they were approaching at an alarming speed, crunching through the crisp foliage, stopping outside the cabin door. My stomach turned over. I stifled a scream. Carefully, I tip-toed toward the gun and removed it from the rack. Whatever was behind that door better start praying.

"Who's there?" I asked.

At first, nothing happened. Then I heard the voice of a woman.

"Lucas," she whispered, from all around me.

I stumbled backwards, as if drunk. I regained my composure, then pointed the gun at the door.

"Identify yourself! Or I'll blow you straight to hell!"

I gripped the gun with cold certainty: I was going to kill something.

The voice spoke again, only this time more forcefully: "Lucas."

"I know my own name."

Something crashed outside the door. That was all it took.

BANG!

The shotgun blast took a huge chunk of the door with it. My ears shattered. After the dust settled, I peeked outside. Nobody was there. Nor were there any track marks. Just mud and trees and lake. A lone wolf cried out, shattering the silence. The loneliness of its howling made me weep.

"I must be losing it," I said, wiping the stream of fresh tears from my face.

I shook my head. That's not true. I'd already lost it. That's what brought me out here in the first place. I regarded my decimated door with utter disdain, then shivered. The bitter breeze wafting into the cabin was unwelcoming. Without a second thought, I fetched some tarpaulin and duct tape from the shed and went to work patching the door. It took the better part of an hour, but it did the trick.

Fatigue held me in its tiresome grip. Meanwhile, my ears continued their incessant ringing from the weapon's discharge. Wearily, I sprawled out on the couch, and for the first time since arriving, I slept soundly.

Day Four:

I woke up well-rested, ready to roll. A speckle of pale light sprinkled into the cabin, as did a newfound sense of purpose: Nothing was going to stop me from completing this album.

"If I really push myself," I said, while loading the coffee maker. "I could finish the album today."

This was true. But I'd have to go hard. I could mix the rest of the songs at home. I opened my laptop, ready to get started, and was surprised by a crimson face flashing across the screen. Its primordial eyes sunk deep into its cheekbones. Its toothy snarl made me cringe. The laptop gurgled, then went blank.

Suddenly, I was frozen with fear. My eyes darted toward the shotgun.

"You haven't lost the nerve, have you?" I asked myself, in a chilling voice.

I shook my head, then forced my attention away from the gun, and instead warmed my hands over the wood stove. My guitar case opened itself. Apparently, I should get back to work. The feeling that I was under a spell was irrefutable.

I strummed an E chord. The sound filled the cabin with rich overtones. As though in a dream, I leaned into the next song: Eyes on You: a weepy ballad about my ex-wife. Halfway through the tune, I felt something tugging forcefully at my leg.

I sprung from my chair in surprise, ruining the take. I swore under my breath. Then I started up again. Although the entire performance was fraught with stabs and jabs from the invisible bystander, and with an endless choir singing along with each chorus, I crushed it.

Without a second thought, I placed my capo on the seventh fret and found my thumb pick; then I ran through a fingerstyle blues with a gospel twist called After the Rain. It would prove to be another first-taker. I was on a roll. The afternoon flew by like a midsummer's dream; and as the evening sun descended across the marmalade sky, and the cascade of stars illuminated the world above me, I finished recording my album.

Soon afterwards, I slept, and was feasted upon by an endless cycle of nightmares.

Day Five:

Morning filled the cabin with light. As the memories of dream-like monsters faded, I forced myself off the couch. Then I gasped. The laptop came alive. That devilish face was speaking in tongues, directly into my head, flashing on and off the screen in seething rage. I jumped so high that I cracked my head on the ceiling, biting my tongue in the process.

In a frenzy, I slammed the laptop shut and started packing up. It didn't take long. I spent the remainder of the day building a new cabin door. Although the shed is stocked with tools and lumber, it was a daunting task. But at least it kept my mind off of the shotgun. And the evil spirits.

Before leaving, I snapped a pic of the guitars leaning lazily against the new cabin door: the beat-to-death Harmony snuggling the glorious Gibson jumbo; a beam of radiant light sprinkling onto the guitars, giving them an angelic appearance. This would prove to be the album cover.

I made it home by nine. With me came a new resolution. A reason for sticking around a wee bit longer. I wanted to show off my new songs. The record company was over the moon. They thought the 'audience' was a clever touch.

I emailed the album art. They could edit it to their liking. Then, using the footage from my iPhone and GoPro, I made a video for Hammer Song, giving it a grainy tinge for ambience, blending closeup guitar bits with the full-cabin experience. The dancing orbs in the background were barely noticeable.

As I was uploading a teaser of the video onto YouTube, an email arrived from the record company:

Great stuff Lucas! Here's the finished album cover. Hope you like it. We certainly do. Big things ahead!

What caught my attention was the name of the album, printed in simple lettering just below my name:

Cabin Fever.

The pic was cropped and colour-boosted. Something else caught my eye: a ghostly face peering out from the crook of the window. The face was eerily familiar. I zoomed in and gasped.

"This makes no sense," I muttered under my breath.

But then again, it made perfect sense. It was my grandmother.

Frog Dissecting Day

It was Frog Dissecting Day. How wonderful. I hate frogs. Always have. Living, dead, makes no difference. They give me the creeps. Yuck. Hideous, slimy, gross creatures. I'd never touched one before, let alone dissected one, and I hoped to keep it that way.

Fat chance.

The classroom smelled worse than road kill. The pungent stench permeated throughout the entire east wing of school. Students covered their mouths, gasping for air, trying to avoid the toxic taste of dead frogs. I don't know why I brought lunch that day, food was the farthest thing from my mind.

To be fair, I wasn't the only cowardly kid. Amanda, the girl sitting next to me, was also turning green. For a moment, I thought she wouldn't make it. I really did. Yet, she maintained her composure, as she sliced open the frog, making horizontal cuts near its arms and legs, removing its liver. She gagged and her legs went wobbly, but her hands were steady. Soon it was over, and she rushed to the washroom, hand-over-mouth, ignoring the snickers coming from kids in the classroom.

Leaving class would be the single best decision of her life.

My embarrassment grew. If she can do it, I can too. I told myself this, but I didn't believe it. Nope, I didn't have the guts. The other students were good to go. They joked as they dissected their ill-fated amphibians, trying to outdo one another. Billy, the class bully and all-around nuisance, wore his frog as a hat, letting the gooey slime slither down his face before licking it up. Once he held the classroom's attention, Billy started speaking in French, talking like a poet. Yeah, Billy's a jerk. (More about him later.)

I stood over the lizardly carcass, trying not to puke. It looked like a giant avocado, with scaly skin, lumpy legs, and beady eyes daring me to go through with it. The putrid stench lodged itself in my throat - every breath was like inhaling sewer gas. It was inescapable. Unfortunately, this wasn't my main concern. My frog looked different from the others. Not only did it stink, but something within its abdomen was stirring. If I wasn't so goddamn scared and ashamed, I might've spoken up.

"Just nerves," I told myself. "I'm squeamish." And that's putting it mildly. My mind went sideways. What's the point of this? How will dissecting this helpless amphibian benefit my future self?

Quick answer: It won't.

My mind was made up: There's no chance in hell I was gonna dissect that frog. No. Fucking. Way. "It's dead," my rational self replied. "It won't feel a thing." Uh-uh. Not happening.

The teacher told me to hurry up. The rest of the class was waiting. All eyes turned and stared. Sweat beat down my brow. The minutes felt like hours.

Scissors in hand, I gazed solemnly at the dead frog. My hands were shaky. Tears filled the corners of my eyes. All I had to do was tear it open and remove its guts. Then this nightmare will be over. I hesitated. This was proving more difficult than expected.

Then I noticed something dreadful: The entire class was giggling, mocking me with their hurtful eyes. Billy was making jokes at my expense, to everyone's delight. Even the teacher was annoyed. I could see it in Miss Taylor's eyes; 'Oh look, the weird kid's acting weird again.'

The other frogs lay in pans, gutted and gazed upon. I was the only one left: The scaredy cat. Ugh. Could my life be any more miserable? "I should never have taken this class," I told myself, shaking in my shoes. "I belong in drama class, not this."

Last year, I was lucky. We were dissecting worms; long and squiggly things, purple and puss-filled. Keith Emery, my science partner did the cutting, while I pretended to watch. Oh, what a relief that was. I prayed it would happen again this year.

It didn't.

The frog was staring up at me, dead and bloated. What caught my attention – more like made my skin crawl – was how much it had grown. By now, it looked like an overstuffed burrito. It could barely fit inside the pan. Not only that, it was pulsating. Dead things don't pulsate. Do they?

Unbeknownst to me, something horrific was about to be birthed. Something that would change my entire view of reality. With the weight of the world resting on my shoulders, and the entire class waiting, I soldiered on.

"Okay," I said aloud, not caring that they could hear me. "Let's get this over with."

The steely utensils glistened under the fluorescent lights. My heart was in my mouth. My legs could barely hold the weight of my body. I wiped the stream of snot sliding down my face with my sleeve; then with trembling hands, I gripped the cold dissecting scissors and jammed them into the frog.

It exploded!

Guts and gore erupted from the amphibian, covering me head to toe. Chunks of fatty flesh slithered down my face, warm and wet and gross. I was draped in thick, greenish-red goop. Some of it slid into my mouth, squishy like toothpaste. Panicking, I forced my fingers into my mouth and pulled out a fucking eyeball.

It blinked.

The classroom shrieked.

Miss Taylor tried restoring order, but it was no use. Mayhem ensued. To everyone's horror, the mound of mucus that was my frog, was slithering along the classroom floor, collecting shape, until it formed a blob. Its head was huge, with narrow eyes and cauliflower ears; its big round body was a mass of sickly skin, groaning as it expanded, until it was the size of a large dog.

It roared its disapproval; a guttural noise, sending shock waves throughout the classroom, causing panic. The teacher shuffled through her desk, cursing in quiet despair, as her disobeying hands let her phone slip through her fingers. She tripped and fell backwards, straight into the jaws of the egregious green blob.

Miss Taylor was devoured. Legs as long as Texas disappeared inside the belly of the beast, clicking red heels and all. Her bones snapped and crackled; her blood splashing across the chalkboard like fresh paint.

Nobody moved.

Tasha Gruber, a straight-A student whom everyone adored, cried out suddenly. The blob quickly turned. With its T-Rex arms, it stuffed her inside its ginormous mouth, kicking and screaming. The blob's wart-infested tongue expanded; its mouth wide open, exposing a tray of razor-sharp teeth, which bit off Tisha's head. Her body plonked, then was viciously eaten. Tasha was gone, but her blood was everywhere.

Billy reacted first: Standing on his desk, camera in hand, filming, he told the creature to eat a dick. The classroom held its breath. Then with death-defying speed, the blob pounced. Billy flew from the desk, smashing his head on the floor.

"Wha? Is that all ye got?" Billy spat.

The blob attacked Billy.

Billy kicked and clawed, cussing like a pirate. Fighting the creature. Then it steamrolled over him. Billy's bones snapped, as his brains splattered across the cold classroom floor. The creature stuffed Billy into its moist mouth. Then it swallowed.

I wasn't the only one who pissed himself.

(To be fair, it's not everyday a creature emerges from a dead frog's belly and starts eating a classroom of kids. Nobody knew what to do. (And it was MY FROG! *What kind of frog was this? Normal frogs don't birth killer green blob, do they?*)

With Billy dead and gone, the beastly blob blasted over a flurry of classmates in the span of seconds. It snapped like a crocodile, ripping the kids apart, feasting on flesh and bone, before swallowing. Then it stopped.

By now it was as big as Godzilla.

Nobody moved.

A rumbling noise came gurgling deep within its bowels; the beast's belly was bulging like a balloon. The entire class stood petrified, watching it gave birth. The smell was unforgivable. Gigantic lumps of goo evacuating from its mouth and anus, as the hideous monster procreated.

Suddenly, there were six of them. And they were hungry. People panicked. Classmates fell or fainted or went into shock.

The brave kids made a mad dash to the door. A lucky pair of girls managed to escape, but the other escapees perished. The slithering slabs feasted fully upon their arms and legs and blood and brains. Nothing was left out. Not even their backpacks.

The school bell rang.

The room gasped, and pale faces gawked.

The blobs regrouped; their gaping mouths wet with drool, as they slithered.

Suddenly, what was left of the class, was looking at me to do something. Like this was my fault. The creatures crept closer, slobbering and full of fangs. With hesitation, I grabbed the scalpel off the floor, edging toward the window, trying to be invisible.

The band of blobs belched up buckets of blood. Then they fed. One by one, the unholy creatures gobbled up my classmates, drinking their tears. They killed quick and smartly. I watched in horror as Tessa Lockhart, who I'd known since the second grade, was bludgeoned to death, swallowed by a baby blob. All that remained was a strand of golden hair, as long as an eagle's feather.

I was now the last kid standing. All my classmates were dead. Nothing remained but their names. My back was against the wall. I was surrounded by snarling blobs, drool dripping down their spongy faces. I was about to be inhaled by the unhallowed beings, spurting saliva that came out of my dissected frog.

To my dismay, I stood frozen.

The blobs were making those noises again. Their slimy skin jiggling as they groan. Right before my very eyes, yet another army of blobs was being birthed. Blobs belching out more blobs. The classroom was in disarray: desks overturned, bile and blood.

An army of blobs faced me, snarling. I gulped. Surely, this can't be happening.

CRASH.

I fell. Wind whipped my face. The fresh air tasted like sex. My eyes snapped open. The window was smashed; a firefighter with giant-sized hockey gloves reached in and grabbed hold of me, forcing me to my feet.

"Come quick!" the firefighter ordered.

Next thing I know, I'm being dragged through the window, slicing my head and shoulders. Behind me, the blobs continued to multiply. It sounded like an orgy of the worst kind. Once outside, I dropped to my knees and wept. Who knew the air could taste so sweet?

I was rushed to the hospital.

Things got even weirder.

First off, it wasn't a normal hospital. Not even close. This was a government quarantine facility. It was colorless and cold. Days became weeks, as doctors in astronaut suits administered a series of tests, each worse than the last. I was strapped to a bed, drained of my blood, fed through tubes, and poked and prodded in places I'd rather not confess. This went on and on. Over time, I wished the blobs had eaten me. Anything to rid myself of these awful experiments.

Oh, sweet irony. Now I was the test frog.

I was scanned with weird machines, cooked like meat, and forced drugs that induced hallucinations beyond my most terrifying nightmares. At some point, I gave up all hope of ever returning to the real world. That this would never end.

But alas, I was released.

Although my time at the facility remains a blur, I do remember the cops. Their questions came like rapid fire, wanting to know everything that happened that fateful day. Apparently, the cameras inside the classroom were destroyed, and the girls that got away were too traumatized to testify.

This was a big story for awhile. Now nobody talks about it. Truth told: I wanna put this behind me. Start living again. Maybe one day I'll write a book. Yeah, that would be cool: Alien blob Creatures Invade Classroom.

Whatever became of the blobs?

I dunno. But there's one thing I am certain of: I'll never EVER dissect another frog.

The Monster At The Bottom Of The Lake

I was twenty when I almost drowned in a lake. I was with my college buddies when it happened. Stupidly, we overloaded Joe's small fishing boat with supplies, and the boat capsized. But something else happened on the lake that day. Something which I've never spoken of. The monster at the bottom of the lake nearly killed me. Twenty-five years later, it's calling out to me again.

We were up north when it happened. (When I say up north, I'm talking 600 miles north of Toronto. So, yeah, north.) Me and Daniel were visiting our buddy Joe and his girlfriend Trina up in Kapuskasing that summer; we were looking to catch us some walleye and lake sturgeon, and have ourselves a good time doing so.

We spent the afternoon fishing along the Kapuskasing River with mild-to-adequate success. Joe knew of a secret camping spot on an anonymous lake where the fish were always biting. He convinced us to go. It's an hour north of Kap, he said, in the middle of Nowheresville. This was a new world for me and Daniel, who've never been this far north, and we were as green as the moss which seemed to be growing on everything we touched.

We required Joe's aluminium fishing boat to transport us to the small islet. Needless to say, we over-packed the boat. We had three tents, two acoustic guitars, two coolers full of food, four cases of beer, fold-up chairs and a plethora of fishing paraphernalia, not to mention life jackets, bug spray, tarp, strong weed and plenty of smokes. From all accounts, it started out as a fun weekend.

We partied and jammed on the guitars and sang drunkenly all night long, blanketed by the stars in the endless, northern sky. When it was fully dark, we sat transfixed around the campfire while Joe regaled us with scary stories regarding the monster living at the bottom of the lake. These stories, it is said, go back many generations. The monster, Joe told us under the waning light of the crescent moon, has habituated this lake for aeons, long before any settlers dared to occupy this frigid, northerly land. Sometimes the monster gets hungry. That's when people go missing. Every year some poor fisherman goes missing at this lake, and no body is ever found. It's why the locals rarely, if ever, fish here. The lake may be small, Joe said, but it's deep.

I thought he was telling tall tales, you know? I was dead wrong. The following day, after enjoying a delicious dinner of smoked pickerel, fried potatoes and corn, Joe decided it was time to pack up the boat and head home, before it gets dark.

Once again, the boat was bogged down with our supplies. We all knew this was dangerous, but we did it anyway. To make matters worse, nobody knew we were here. Remember, this was the 90's – before smartphones – so it wasn't uncommon for people to disappear on fishing trips. Just ask Bill Barilko. We spotted one other boater on the lake that day, a fisherman, and that was early in the morning. As far as we knew, we had this body of water to ourselves. It was after seven by the time we set our sad little vessel back into the water. Soon the sun would set and things would go wonky.

I remember it clearly: Joe and Trina were situated at the back of the boat; Joe was struggling, as he guided the vessel across the bumpy lake. The boat wanted none of it. We were constantly being knocked back and forth, as if on a wooden roller coaster, and I could tell Joe was nervous, something I'd never seen before. Daniel sat at the bow; his job was to monitor the water level getting into our boat. This was an important job. Poor Daniel was in full panic mode from the get-go. "We should never have put so much stuff in the boat," he complained, over and over, while spooning the water out of the boat. Of course, he was correct, but we were young and carefree and hopelessly naïve.

The lake was furious. Whitecaps rolled angrily across the entire bowl of water. Water was seeping into the boat at an alarming rate. I was sitting in the middle of the boat, doing little of value, watching as the anxiety on Daniel's face intensified. We were now at the middle of the lake, the water was a foot deep inside the boat, and the lake continued to pound us into submission. To make matters worse, only a speckle of sunlight remained. Time, as they say, was of the essence.

Joe boated us laboriously across the water as best he could. Our vessel was teetering dangerously low due to our negligence, and the whitecaps continued to submerge the boat. Daniel was having a panic attack. I'll never forget the look of pure, unadulterated terror on Daniel's long, pale face that final moment before we sank the boat.

"Joe!" he said. "Joe! Help!"

Those were his final words. His eyes were big and round and full of fear. He was frantically scooping the water out of the boat using a discarded tin can, but his efforts were futile. One minute we were floating haphazardly across the drink, the next moment we were underwater. The boat capsized. Our belongings either sank to the bottom of the lake or floated away. First, we removed our footwear; I was sad to see my Doc Martins fall to the bottom of the lake, then we scrounged up the life jackets and put them on nice and snug. We then spent a good fifteen minutes trying to flip the boat over, right-side-up, but failed. Instead, we wasted precious time and energy.

Daniel, who was the most scared, was quickly becoming unnerved. It was sad to see. Trina, on the other hand, swam Olympian-style across the lake and reached shore twenty minutes later. Joe trailed close behind her. Neither of them hesitated. They just went for it.

It was now me and Daniel stuck out in the middle of the lake. The City Slickers. Neither of us were sufficient swimmers. Daniel was going into shock. "Just swim!" I told him. I was trying to sound brave. Truth is, I can't swim to save my life, I never could, but with the life jacket on, I was willing to at least give it a shot. I could see Joe and Trina waving to us from shore, but barely. The sun was sinking fast. In twenty minutes or so we'll be covered in a shroud of darkness. Then what? I feared the worst. I swam like my life depended on it. If Trina and Joe can do it, I can too. Yes, I'm a lousy swimmer, but goddammit, I swam. At some point I looked behind me to check on Daniel, and to my horror, he was swimming backstroke, going the wrong way.

"Dan!" I called out. "You're going the wrong way!"

He didn't hear me. And I was growing weak and weary. My arms and legs were dead tired. I was frightfully cold. My time was coming to an end; I realised this joylessly. I strained to see the spec of land off in the distance, where Trina and Joe were waiting for us. Soon the shore would disappear completely and they would too.

Something nudged my foot. Must be a fish, I told myself. A big one. I shook my leg, hoping to shoo it off. Then it happened again, only more forcibly. I started kicking my legs, looking to scare off whatever it was. It didn't work. Suddenly, I was scared. Something was underneath me. Something big. It latched onto my leg. It didn't let go. It forced me under water. Frantically, I fought to free myself from whatever it was. I had no idea what was happening. Moments later, I came up coughing and wheezing, gasping for air. By this point I was out of my mind, terrified.

"Dan!" I shouted. My voice sank like a stone. "Dan! There's something down there!"

I swam to him. It took all my strength to do so. He was crying. Something snatched my foot again; something brittle, like sandpaper. I felt its teeth. My leg was getting torn to shreds. The pain was uncompromising.

"Wh-what the hell was that?" I asked, through chattering teeth. The look stamped across Daniel's face said everything I needed to know. He'd felt it too. "There's something down there," I said. "We gotta get moving."

We swam. Unfortunately, the lake was non-compliant, and our efforts were futile. There was no use. We were both incompetent swimmers. The lake had us all to itself. Us, and the monster at the bottom of the lake. Daniel straightened out, and for a moment, I thought we had a fighting chance at reaching shore. Then he got pulled under.

"Dan!" He was gone. I began splashing and making an abundance of noise. "Dan!" Something grabbed my leg. Plunk, I went under.

I died. I'm sure of this. A bright light was tunnelling toward me. I went toward the light, and for a moment I was at peace. Then everything came rushing in. My lungs filled with lake water, my body was thrashing about. Something was dragging me to the bottom of the lake. I opened my eyes. For a moment, all I could see was the murkiness of lake water; then I saw it: The monster.

It took a moment to comprehend what I was witnessing. The monster was huge. It looked like a giant otter, only uglier. It had beady eyes, elongated whiskers and long, muscular arms with stringy claws. And teeth. I remember those teeth well; sharp, white, crooked and cruel. Beside me was Daniel; he was missing his left arm. Blood was pouring out of him like paint from a can. His eyes were open and lifeless. I fought the beast as best I could; unfortunately, my strength was at zero, and I was towed to the bottom of the lake.

The monster, easily twice my size and weight, held me in a bear hug. I could feel my vertebra being crushed. Resistance seemed futile by this point. This is how I was going to die. I succumbed. Then I snapped out of it. I became alert. Just as my lungs were about to burst, I fought the monster with everything I had. I went ballistic. I jerked and lurched and scratched and flailed about. I had no shame. Without warning, it released me, and I shot back up to the surface like a torpedo.

The fresh air was better than sex. I took a moment to marvel in its wonder, then I began searching for Daniel. I couldn't see him anywhere. By this point, I'm still struggling to catch my breath. Plus, I was terrified of whatever it was at the bottom of the lake, and expecting to be hauled back down at any moment. My life jacket was torn to shreds, rendering it impotent. I was going to drown. Then I heard a noise and my heart almost exploded. I looked up and saw a thin spec of light from another boat: the fisherman from earlier this morning, I was saved!

Within minutes I was discovered; the fisherman hauled me into his boat. He offered me some hot coffee from his cooler. It tasted delicious. By this time the darkness had arrived, along with the bugs, which were ravenous, but I didn't care, I was alive.

I told him about Daniel. The look on the fisherman's face was not encouraging, but to his credit, we combed the lake for over an hour, only to come up empty-handed. My mind was still grappling with what just transpired. Should I tell this man about the monster in the bottom of the lake? Would he believe me? Would anyone believe me, for that matter? Or would they think I was crazy. Ultimately, I didn't mention the monster at the bottom of the lake. I mean, who would?

...

It's been many years since that fateful summer on the lake, and I haven't spoken about this to a single soul. Although we did manage to fish my acoustic guitar from the lake (it never played the same since), Daniel's body was never found. He never did get the chance at finishing med school and becoming a surgeon, as was his plan. It was tragic. His family, as you can imagine, was overwhelmed with grief.

Recently, I received an email from Joe, wanting me to visit him and Trina up in Kapuskasing. It's been too long, he said. Joe, who still loves the great outdoors, is as jaunty as ever. 'We should go camping at the lake,' Joe said in his email. 'We'll take the kids and the guitars and the fishing rods and we'll have ourselves a blast. Catch us some dinner while we're at it.'

Reluctantly, I agreed.

As I venture up to the attic of Ontario, I'm reminded again of the monster at the bottom of the lake. I hadn't thought of that lake-bound beast in many years, except in my dreams (only in my dreams I always end up as monster food). Now I can't get the water-ogre out of my mind. There's a monster living at the bottom of the lake, the locals say, but of course it can't be real. I'm a fully-grown adult now. I don't believe in such folklore. This is my mantra.

Apparently, the locals have since made tee-shirts celebrating the lake monster: WE DON'T FEED THE MONSTER – THAT'S WHAT CITY SLICKERS DO. Classy. I'll be sure to wear mine as we drop Joe's dinghy into that frigid, northern lake. Winter's fast approaching so we'll need to dress extra warm. Legend has it, the monster gets extra hungry this time of year. Lucky me. I still can't swim.

Chicken Coop Massacre

"Go feed them chickens," Ma said, sourly. "And bring back some eggs while yer at it."

It was a bitter October morning. Despite the cold, I hurried outside to do my chores, as I do most mornings. Doing chores doesn't bother me; I love the chicks, especially Birdman, the grumpy ol' rooster. He's my alarm clock.

This particular morning, however, Birdman didn't wake me up, which was weird. I'd never slept in before. Something was wrong. Me and Ma live in the middle of nowhere, when strange stuff things happen, it usually means trouble.

Then I saw the blood.

My beloved Birdman was decapitated. His lifeless carcass left to rot, while the other chicks ambled about unprovoked. Strange thing was, the chicken coop, which my father built two summers ago just before Ma kicked him out, was untampered. There were no track marks, no signs of tampering or tunnelling. Just blood. But whatever killed poor ol' Birdman was merciless. Wringed his neck good.

I ran inside and told Ma, who got mad at me, like it was my fault or something.

"You didn't lock the coop," Ma snapped. "How many times do I hafta tell ya? Lock that friggin door at night!"

Ma ain't no Mary Poppins, if you catch my drift.

I scratched my head, knowing full well it was locked. This made no sense. I was thirteen, not stupid. The coop was locked. I was sure of it.

Ma fetched her shotgun and searched the yard, daring whoever – or whatever – was out there to show its face. When she came back, she was furious.

"Bury the bird," Ma ordered.

I leaned in, about to complain.

"Alexandria. Now!"

I fetched the shovel and went.

You see, Ma only calls me Alexandria when she's seriously pissed off. I frowned. If Pa were here, he'd do it. Pa ain't scared of nothing. Certainly not scared of poor ol' Birdman, dead and decapitated, sticky with blood.

Pouting like a kid, I scooped up Birdman and carried him to the edge of the yard. Then I buried him. It was sad. Everywhere I looked, I remembered the silly rooster. Like how he would eat from my hand, or how Pa let me name him.

Two days later, it happened again.

Wearily, I went out to feed the flock. Then I stopped, unable to believe my eyes. The chicken coop was a bloodied massacre. The smell of death was pungent; the bloodstained floor was covered in brightly coloured feathers.

"That's impossible!" Ma bellowed, when I told her.

She pushed past me and ran outside, still in her nightgown, to have a look. She brought her shotgun. I watched from the safety of my window, not trusting that look in Ma's eyes, or the carcasses scattered across the coop. So much blood and gore. Each and every chic was dead. Made zero sense. Nothing coulda done that. Nothing I ever seen.

Ma surveilled the property, coming back empty handed, then she told me to bury the birds. Grudgingly, I grabbed the shovel – yet again – and wasted the day digging holes. As I dug, a feeling stole over me: the killer was close, watching me. And I was next. That put a jump in my step. One thing was certain: I didn't want to end up like poor ol' Birdman.

All eleven chicks in the flock were dismembered; some decapitated, others strangled; their tiny, tortured tongues lay leaking from broken yellow beaks. One chick had both legs ripped off, its plumage fouled with feces. It was gruesome. Nothing had prepared me for such wretchedness. I was totally repulsed.

Digging graves is a daunting task, and not without pitfalls. More than once, a chicken head flew from my shovel and rolled away. Ugh. Could this day get any worse? I hoped not. Silently, I prayed for Pa to return home. He'd know what to do.

I was cold and tired and miserable, but I did my chores. All the while, my eyes kept darting towards the coop. The door had been locked, there was no doubt this time. I triple-checked before bed. What kind of monster could mutilate an entire flock, without leaving a trace? Only a ghost could do that.

I slept poorly all week; my mind was on overdrive, longing for clues. Somewhere out there was the killer, lurking in the woods, only to come out at night. The fact that the killer's been in my backyard, twice, gave me the creeps. What if it returns?

Ma bought more chicks, and put an electric fence around the pen, to ward off predators. The new chicks were cute, but I refused to become friends with them. No more heartbreaks. Except, that's not quite true. There was this one particular rooster. He seemed so wise, watching over the others, angelic-like. I named him Allister. Over time he became Alice. What a voice he had. Alice could raise the dead any given morning; he was so loud.

One chilly morning, Alice didn't wake me up. When I got up, Ma was on the phone with the police, talking in circles, pacing the house, stark raving mad. With a heavy heart, I went outside to see what the problem was.

The entire flock was butchered; blood, bones, beaks and brains lay scattered everywhere. I was outraged, wanting to get to the bottom of this. Once again, the coop was undamaged; no tracks, no signs of forced entry, no tunnelling, nothing.

I was stumped, so I called Tammy, my BFF.

Tammy arrived full of spirit, her tote bag full of tools and gadgets. To her this is fun. She led me into the forest, where we started a proper investigation, looking for anything unusual. She was quite thorough. "There must be clues," she repeated, in an excited voice, checking the forest floor for clues.

We spent all day in the woods. A white-tailed deer sauntered passed; it turned and stared, then disappeared into the tall grass. Maybe it was an omen. Tammy said. "These woods are home to eastern coyotes, red foxes and the odd black bear," she told me, matter-of-factly. "But those creatures only come out at night. Entering a chicken coop is one thing, but with an electric fence - and leaving no trace at all?" She too, was stumped.

Tammy stayed for dinner, during which she suggested Ma buy a surveillance camera. Ma agreed.

The next day, Ma went to town to stock up on chickens – yet again – only this time she also brought home a small surveillance camera, which I had the displeasure of setting up.

Ma was worrying me. She was really unglued, paranoid and angry. When I suggested we ask Pa for help, she slapped me.

Finally, the camera was set up, and linked to my phone. I protested, but Ma's phone is older than dirt, she despises technology. The camera was my responsibly, so I'd better get used to it. The first night, I could barely sleep. Every time there was a noise, I rushed to my phone, just in case.

Then one morning, it happened again.

Our entire flock was dismembered. It was a chicken coop massacre. Blood was everywhere, plus random bird parts and bloodstained feathers. Still, no tracks, nor any signs of disruption, as far anyone could tell. Even the cops were baffled. By now, our neighbors – and I use the term loosely, seeing how our closest neighbor was a ten-minute bike ride away – were put on High Alert. This was Big News. Everyone in town was talking about it.

I stayed home from school that day; cleaning up carnage, burying dead birds. Our yard was a friggin' animal graveyard. I was terrified. Even a country bumkin like me knows how these stories end up. Tammy, on the other hand was intrigued, and made me promise to wait before checking the surveillance footage.

After school, Tammy rushed over, then set about scrolling through the surveillance video, until something caught her attention. She stopped suddenly, slack-jawed, bewildered. Then she showed me. "What is it?" she asked, in a faraway voice.

"Whatever it is," I said, scratching my head. "It's bad."

We watched the same scene over and over. At 4:09 am., the creature suddenly appeared outside the coop. With claws and fangs and thick, matted fur, it looked like a werewolf.

The first thing the creature did – I swear to God – was look directly at the camera and wave, but not in a friendly way; more like a I-know-you-can-see-me, and-I-don't-care kind of way.

Then it vanished, reappearing inside the coop, where it murdered the entire flock of chickens one by one, with impossible speed.

"Wait, hold on a second," Tammy said. She played the video at half speed. "Th-that's impossible."

We watched, transfixed, as the creature savagely ripped, clawed and gutted our poultry. The poor chicks didn't know what killed them, it happened so fast. Alice was killed first. The monster reached down and bit its head off; then, in a series of bone-chilling attacks, it slayed the entire flock in similar fashion. The precision of each kill was abhorrent. The entire attack took thirteen seconds.

After the killing spree, the creature made a series of peculiar gestures, as if performing some sort of satanic ritual. Blood dripped from the monster's face, its fangs stained a superlative shade of red. Licking its ruby lips, the creature gazed into the surveillance camera; only this time, I could feel it penetrating my mind. Tammy felt it too. She screamed and locked herself in bathroom and wouldn't come out.

Stupidly, I watched the remainder of the video alone in my bedroom. It was gut-wrenchingly awful. After doing the ritual, the creature touched the top of its head, then it vanished into thin air. As it did, a sardonic voice entered my mind:

You're next, Alexandria.

Panicking, I ran downstairs and showed Ma the video. Problem was, when I tried, there was nothing on the screen but static. "B-b-but, that's impossible," I said, scratching my head.

Ma was fuming, like she wanted to rip my head off. Tammy returned from the bathroom, wiped tears from her freckled face and went home without saying goodbye.

That night, I had a terrible dream; it seemed so real, so vivid, so true: There I was, slaughtering the chickens, crushing their soft skulls with my strong hands; their animal souls plucked from their feathered bodies, as I wrapped my meaty hands around their flimsy necks. One by one, I tore apart the chicks, drinking their blood, and delighting in doing so. Then I crept into the house, where I wrapped my cold, clammy hands around Ma's neck and squeezed. With Ma dead, I appeared outside Tammy's bedroom window, lurking in the dark night, as she slept. The voice was telling me exactly what to do. Tammy wouldn't feel a thing.

I awoke in a pool of sweaty sheets, ravenous. My fingernails were crusted with blood. My arms and legs were sore. Wearily, I crawled out of bed, found my way downstairs, and ate a hearty breakfast. Phew, was I hungry.

The house was library-quiet. Ma must've slept in. This was highly unusual. I tiptoed towards her bedroom door, and waited, too scared to knock. My bloodstained hands were trembling; my legs ready to buckle and fold at any given moment.

"Ma," I said quietly, "Ma, you alright?"

No answer.

I tried again.

Nothing.

Maybe she went into town to gather supplies. Maybe her and Pa were having coffee somewhere. That would be nice.

But I knew better. The roosters hadn't crowed this morning. Not good.

"Ma!" I called out one last time, afraid to peek inside her bedroom. Some places are off limits, no matter what. Then, I remembered the surveillance camera. Maybe I should check it?

Bad idea.

Sure enough, the creature returned, only this time it was at our back door, snarling at the surveillance camera. Horrified, I saw myself inside the creature's eyes. When it spoke my name, I dropped my phone, and ran inside my bedroom, locking the door.

I've been hiding all day, knowing damn-well this is an exercise in futility. But I'm okay with that. First thing's first: remove the blood from my fingernails, before someone sees it. Then, clean up Ma's room. Then it's off to Tammy's place. Something tells me she'll love the creature in the woods.

Let's Make A Deal With The Devil!

"You ready Bruce?" my producer asks, moments before we go live.

"You bet," I say, but it's a lie. I'm not ready. Not after last week's fiasco. How could I be? I check my mirror for any faults in my makeup, suck in my gut, then walk out on stage to a live studio audience.

(Enter music)

The announcer introduces me. I glance down at my monitor and cringe. The producers make me out to be that sleazy game show host from the days of old. Polyester and all.

(Camera one)

We're live.

"Alrighty. I'm happy to be here. Hope you are too!" I say, doing my best Bob Barker impression. "Let's bring out this week's contestant, shall we?" I'm looking at the camera, as if asking the folks at home. "And then…"

(Cue the audience)

"LET'S MAKE A DEAL WITH THE DEVIL!"

This contestant takes to the podium. He's a paunchy, middle-aged man, casually dressed, with broad shoulders and a generous chin. The camera follows him to the podium. Meanwhile, the audience is going berserk.

(Camera two)

"Knock it off!" I tell the audience, playfully. They hush. "Peter McNamara, tell us a little bit about yourself, why don't you?"

(Camera four)

Peter is wiping his sweat-soaked forehead.

"Well Bruce, back in high school, I was leading quarterback for the Mater Dei Monarchs. State Champs, two years running! These days, I mostly sell insurance. Divorced. No kids. Plus…" Saving the best for last, "I'm a lifelong Chargers fan."

Crowd cheers.

(Camera one)

"Alright Peter, are YOU ready to make a DEAL with the DEVIL?"

He was.

"Great! Then let's bring out Damion, shall we?"

(Cue creepy music)

(Split screen)

Damion appears out of nowhere to stand next to Peter.

"Tell me Peter," I ask. "Do you know the rules?"

Peter nods nervously, all the while glancing at the extremely tall man who appeared out of nowhere, and is now standing next to him wearing an outlandish devil suit.

"Great! So, Peter. Tell Damion, and the rest of us, what it is you most desire? Just remember…"

(Cue the audience)

"THE DEVIL'S IN THE DETAILS!"

Peter is shaking like a leaf. His head looks like a well-polished bowling ball.

"Well Bruce," he says. "I've given this a lot of thought."

(Camera three)

"What I really want is a big ol' house on the beach. And a big ol' swimming pool. And a car built like a tank!"

The crowd agrees.

Right away I see the problem. He didn't stick to the script. What's this 'built like a tank' nonsense? Where did that come from? Before each show, I sit down with the contestant and tell them how this works. I tell them exactly what to say, when to say it, and more important: what NOT to say. But the contestants always make a mistake. Every week. One that ultimately costs them their lives, much to the fervor of the audience.

(Camera two)

My pearly white teeth are plastered across the screen.

"Alllright then! Let's ask the devil if he's willing to make a deal, shall we?"

Damion Cary is towering over Peter, grinning like a used car salesman. He looms larger than life, both on and off the screen. Audiences love him. He dresses in a skin tight red leather suit, pointed red tail, pitchfork and devil horns. But don't let his ridiculous attire fool you. It's all a distraction.

Close up of Damion smiling devilishly into the camera.

"Well, well, well. What DO we have here?" Damion asks, in his guttural voice. "Peter, is it? Hmm. I don't know. You ask for so much. But then, you must ask yourself: How badly do you want these things? Are you willing to give your soul?"

Peter would. He really, really would.

"Excellent," Damion sneers, "Just excellent."

(Camera five)

Peter shakes hands with the devil.

I take a cautionary step backward, trying my darnedest not to show fear. I don't want to end up like the previous host. Who would? I cannot let that happen to me. Not while everyone is watching.

(Camera one)

"Well, that's just fabulous! So…"

(Cue audience)

"LET'S MAKE A DEAL WITH THE DEVIL."

Camera four zooms in on Peter, who is sweating profusely, palms clenched, open-mouth smiling.

"That grrreat! But tell me Satan, what's the catch?"

There's always a catch.

"The catch is, Bruce." He leers into the camera with his Don't-Tell-Me-I-Didn't-Warn-You look. "The car will be BIG!

And it'll drive itself! Peter won't have to lift a finger! It'll be a smash!"

Close up of Peter, who appears as happy as a pig in feces.

I hate the next part.

Damion snaps his long and crooked finger – POOF! Peter is gone. Vanished.

The crowd is aghast. They think this is all TV trickery. As the camera cuts to Damion, who's licking his paws and somehow wagging his tail, I recall how the previous host died. I can't get that image out of my head. They're still trying to scrape his stains off the floor, right where I'm standing, no less. But hey: The ratings speak for themselves. Give the people what they want.

Damion is doing his devil shtick and the audience is applauding him. Millions of viewers are watching, waiting for the inevitable carnage that will soon unfold. Meanwhile, the knots in my stomach are multiplying, my left leg is shaking, I'm stone-cold terrified.

Cut to a beach house, where a group of partiers appear on the screen, showing off their California tans, sipping exotic drinks from colorful straws, while they lounge around a large swimming pool in skimpy outfit.

Cut to Peter, who's got a drink in each hand and a shit-eating grin stamped across his face. Peter has become the embodiment of the American Dream right before our eyes.

The audience rages on.

I shutter. My stomach fills with butterflies. I know what's coming. If I screw this next part up, I'll see my career in Hell.

(Camera One)

"Sooo, Peter. Tell the audience at home: How does it feel to finally have your dream home on the beach?"

(Overhead camera)

Peter is happy, as the girls in the background are whooping and hollering and splashing about.

"I'll tell you what, Bruce," he says, sipping his drink, enjoying the view. "It feels great!"

What comes next will haunt me at night, when the lights are off and the cameras put away. Some things in life are impossible to forget. Even for heartless Hollywood vampire types like myself.

(Cut to Damion)

The Devil is standing next to me, too-close-for-comfort.

"Well Peter," his voice, sardonic and cruel. "I can see you like the swimming pool. You DO like the swimming pool, DON'T YOU?"

Close up of Peter grinning ear to ear.

"Gooood. Well then," Damion says, licking his moist red lips. "Let's cut to the chase. I think it's time to bring out THE NEW CAR!"

Damion snaps his finger and a shiny new Hummer appears in the driveway. He's standing next to it dangling a golden set of keys.

I have no clue how he does this. Or where those cameras come from. I'm not allowed to ask, which is fine by me. Some things are best unknown.

Zoom in on Peter, running arms-out to the driveway, carrying his fruit filled drinks. The audience oohs and ahs.

Wide shot of Damion and Peter, standing toe-to-toe in front of the Hummer. The Hummer glistens under the warm California sun.

"You asked for a big car, am I right?" Damion asks, in a bombastic voice.

"Um, yes Damion, I did."

"Well? Is this one big enough?"

Peter nods approvingly.

"Excellent! So, what do ya say, Peter? Wanna take her for a ride?"

Peter does.

Damion snaps his finger. Suddenly he and Peter are inside the Hummer, seat belts and all. Peter's drinks are nowhere to be seen.

People at home think this is studio trickery. It isn't. Which is why I'm shaking.

(Dashboard camera)

Damion is outwardly pleased. He leans into the camera.

"Good. Because…"

(Cue the audience)

"THE DEVIL'S IN THE DETAILS!"

They speed off. Peter's head thrusts back, as they tear out of the driveway onto the busy beach-side boulevard. Damion is smiling, stone-cold murder searing in his eyes.

(Helicopter cam)

The audience watches with glee as the murder spree plays out. First, the Hummer guns down a beautiful young woman on roller blades, blindsiding her.

Her body disappears, as the perilous vehicle effortlessly runs her over. Blood splashes across its shiny chrome grill, as though biting into a strawberry full of razor blades.

The audience is bloodthirsty, wanting more.

(Dashboard cam)

Peter looks worse than I feel. He's freaking out.

Damion's face lights up.

"You're gonna love this next part. Peter!"

(Multi-screen heli-cams)

Hummer veers left onto the sandy beach. A man's head gets crushed like a grape; his brains splatter across his finely-chiselled chest. His left eyeball rolls away, lost in the many crevasses of the crimson sand, while his lifeless body lie flattened on his blood-soaked beach towel.

Beside him, a figure rests in twisted ruins with tire tracks tattooed across his sun-kissed corpse. His arm dangles futilely from its socket, like a noose swaying in the breeze.

The third victim is caught in the grill of the Hummer. It does a few back flips as the vehicle comes to a halt. Its body falls limply into the warm sand and stays there: blood and body parts and suntan lotion and all.

(Camera two)

Sweating, I'm doing my darnedest to appear casual.

"Incredible stuff, Damion," I say, wearing my stapled-on smile. "That was one heck of a bargain you got there, Peter. Does the audience agree with me or what?"

They do.

"Goood. I hope each and every one of you at home agrees too."

Cut to Damion, who's somehow back in the studio, standing at the podium next to me, twirling his long devil tail, smug as a bug on a rug. His eyes meet mine and fill me with dread.

Close up of me.

My leg refusing to stay still.

"L-let's see how things are going with Peter, shall we?"

Wide-shot of the beach. The scene is horrific. Police everywhere, trying to regulate the manic crowd who moments ago, were enjoying a picturesque afternoon on the beach.

Camera zooms in on the girl wearing roller blades lying face down in a pool of blood. Her neck snapped like a twig, her bleach-blonde hair slathered in blood and tiny specs of brain.

(Multi-cam)

Peter from every angle tumbles out of the Hummer.

The cops arrive in droves.

All at once, every bullet in America is pointed at him. He's crying; phlegm and snot flowing from his ruby-red nose like honey from a razor's edge. The cops are giving him orders but he doesn't seem to notice. Instead, he's fumbling for his keys, talking gibberish.

His keys slip from his fingers.

The audience is biting their nails.

(Multi-Cam)

Multi-cam shows me trying not to vomit. I'm holding it back as best I can. The show's almost over, I tell myself. I can make it through this. I must. Then I'm safe; until next week, that is.

Close-up of Peter reaching for his keys.

That's the last thing he'll ever do.

Multi-cam shows Peter from every possible angle, as a banquet of bullets pulverize his flesh and bone. He flounders like a bloody rag doll as his brains explode into a million pieces, like ravioli hitting a fan. Then he falls flat on his bullet-ridden face. That's the end of Peter McNamara.

The audience rages on.

(Camera one)

Close up of me, ghost-white, shaking like a leaf.

"It looks like Peter got the WRONG END OF THAT BARGAIN!"

Much applause.

(Cue music)

(Camera one)

"W-well folks," I say. "B-be sure to tune in next week. And try and have yourself a good night. I look forward to seeing you again next week, on..."

(Cue audience)

"LET'S MAKE A DEAL WITH THE DEVIL!"

Let's Make A Deal With The Devil!
Season 2 Premiere:

"You ready Bruce?"

"Ready as I'll ever be."

Except, I'm not ready. How can I be? I barely survived Season One. And the Season Finale was a disaster. Poor contestant was burned to a crisp. Smelled like burnt chicken and rotten eggs.

"Quiet on the set!"

I suck in my gut.

"Going live in five… four… three… two…"

(Cue creepy music)

(Camera one)

I get the nod.

"Hello out there, wherever you are. Welcome to Season Two of…"

(Cue audience)

"LET'S MAKE A DEAL WITH THE DEVIL."

(Camera three)

I tease the audience.

"Alright, alright. Knock it off!"

I check my watch.

"My name is Bruce Davie, and I'm terrified…I mean… happy to be here. Alright, now that the formalities are over, lets bring out today's contestant, shall we?"

Audience applauds.

(Camera four)

A generous woman wearing yoga pants and a loose-fitting Lynyrd Skynyrd tee-shirt appears on screen. She fist-pumps across the stage.

I roll my eyes. Where do they find these people?

(Split screen)

"Tell us a bit about yourself, starting with who you are and where you're from."

I look directly into the camera, raise an eyebrow.

"But please, make it brief. We wouldn't want to keep the Devil waiting, would we?"

The audience oohs and ahs.

The heavily tattooed woman shakes her head.

"Good to be here, Bruce. I just love…"

She flaps her meaty arms in the air.

(Cue audience)

"LET'S MAKE A DEAL WITH THE DEVIL."

I shake my head, then immediately straighten up. Mustn't stray from the script. Maybe, just maybe, I can save her from a gruesome fate.

(Camera four)

"Name's Bertha. Bertha Squires. Folks back home call me Big Bertha. I'm from the great state of Georgia."

She shakes, crowd roars.

"And I like beers and barbecued ribs, and Lynyrd Skynyrd played real loud. And I loooove the Falcons. Let's go Falcons!"

The audience cheers.

"Alright, alright," I say, signalling the audience to simmer down. "Let's get down to business, shall we? I do believe it's time to…"

(Cue audience)

"BRING OUT THE DEVIL."

(Cue creepy music)

The lights flicker. Minty fog stretches across the studio. An illuminated pentagram flashes above the audience, much to their delight.

My stomach sinks into my toes. I hate this part. Damion doesn't take part in the rehearsals. He appears only when the cameras are rolling. Although on occasion, his deep, guttural voice wafts from the producer's office. Like today, when I overheard them discussing the future of the show. My name wasn't mentioned.

Fire flashes across the stage.

Damion suddenly appears.

The audience gasps.

(Camera three)

Closeup of Damion wearing his elaborate, skin-tight red devil suit. His leather tail swings confidently, to the delight of our viewers. Apparently, Hell beings get one hour of leisure time a week, and they love this show. How they get this small-scale show in the first place is beyond me. Maybe Hell has good WiFi.

Damion tilts his black fedora, then he extends an arm, hushing the audience.

"Good evening!"

The audience applauds.

Damion smiles slyly, showcasing his gold-tooth display.

"So, Bertha," he exaggerates her name. "Let's cut to the chase. Tell me… no tell the viewers… what it is you most desire?"

(Split screen)

The Devil sneers.

Bertha puffs out her chest.

"Well Damion, I want what every American wants."

The audience leans in.

"Mo money!"

The audience jumps to their feet, cheering.

(Camera one)

I see myself in the monitors, looking small and insignificant.

"Alright, alright," I say shakily. "I'm sure Damion can manage that. After all, he IS the Devil."

(Enter creepy music)

(Camera three)

Damion licks his lips.

"Excellent," he says, fiddling his fingers. "I can certainly arrange that."

(Camera four)

Bertha starts fist-pumping, to the audience's delight.

"But first," Damion sneers. "You must sign a contract. Then it's official."

He snaps his fingers.

The sound ricochets across the studio like a thunderclap.

Suddenly, he's holding an ancient-looking contract made of human skin. I'll be damned if the words aren't written in blood.

I shudder.

(Split screen)

Damion hands her the contract.

The contestant places the parchment on to the pedestal; a pool of sweat glistens from her gleaming forehead.

Damion's eyes sparkle like oceans of evil.

Big Bertha winces as he touches her arm.

The Devil turns to the audience.

"Whatcha think?" His voice sounds like an ashtray. "Should Big Bertha become America's next billionaire?"

"Hell yeah!" Bertha raises her mighty arms. "Lord, let the money rain over me!"

The audience agrees.

I shrink into my shoes. Could this get any worse?

(Camera four)

"Excellent."

Damion snaps his spidery fingers. Suddenly, he's holding a quilted pen.

"Sign here, here and…."

He's making a mockery of this.

"Initial here."

Cautiously, Bertha takes the pen.

"But read through it carefully. Because…"

(Cue audience)

"THE DEVIL'S IN THE DETAILS."

Bertha's round face turns scarlet. Her beady eyes show a mixture of terror and greed.

(Split screen)

The devil licks his lizardly lips.

The audience holds its breath.

The contract trembles in the contestant's hands.

Yawning, Damion taps his Rolex, giving the camera a million-dollar grin.

"Hurry it up, wouldya? We're on live television!"

The audience chants: "SIGN IT… SIGN IT… SIGN IT…"

Close up of the contestant leaning over, about to sign.

"Uh huh." Damion snaps his fingers; a bottle of ink appears.

The contestant dips the pen into the jar of red ink.

The audience rises to its feet.

The contestant signs the contract.

(Camera one)

My game-show-host smile is stapled to my face.

"Well done, Bertha. You've just made a deal with the Devil!"

The audience goes ballistic.

(Camera pans out)

Grinning grotesquely, Damion flies above the audience, whose necks are stretched like cranes.

(Close up of the Devil)

"I, the one known as Lucifer, the truly wicked one, proclaims…." His arms stretch across the entire studio. "Let it rain cold, hard, cash!"

The audience is delirious.

Thunder crashes. Shots ring out.

Everyone screams, including me. This wasn't part of the script. But then again, when does Damion follow the script?

(Camera five)

The Devil snaps his long finger.

The studio dissolves into dust. Suddenly, instead of being inside a cheap Hollywood studio, we're packed inside a football stadium. The smell of stale beer and popcorn prevails.

I stumble; my heart threatens to explode. I clutch my chest, fearing the worst. My face turns red, then green, then settles on pale-white.

Damion gives me his do-as-I-say look, then points up.

Looking up, my stomach fills with dread. A lone, greenback cascades from the sky, landing on the contestant's head. She snatches it, stuffs it between her big breasts.

More money falls. Within seconds, the stadium fills with cash. Big Bertha gets down to business.

Damion flies across the stadium, singing, "Let it rain, let it rain, let it rain." His dreadful voice comes through the stadium speakers.

Pandemonium ensues.

(Overhead camera)

Like a plague of locusts, money plummets into the stadium.

The audience is on their feet, seizing the cash. Kicking and clawing, biting and scratching, they line their pockets with cash.

The Devil snaps his fingers.

Almost immediately, the downpour turns torrential. A never-ending flow of cash is dropped into the stadium. The air turns dark, difficult to breathe.

People panic.

(Camera two)

My game show-host smile is slipping. With all my might, I finally speak.

"I've heard of it raining cats and dogs, but this is ridiculous!"

Meanwhile, my legs are trapped under three feet of cash. I'm losing my equilibrium.

(Camera three)

Damion hovers over the contestant, who's waist-deep in cash, and offers her money bags.

"Fill em up!" he shouts.

(Split screen)

Bertha snatches the money bags, starts filling them with cash.

Audience members, the lucky ones seated at the top, are chanting: "FILL THEM UP… FILL THEM UP…"

Contestant appears on the jumbo screen.

She's desperate, unable to keep up with the rising tides. The storm of green shows no sign of letting up, and she's getting the worst of it.

(Overhead camera)

The storm turns into an avalanche. The entire front row is crushed. Their screams are inaudible over the madness.

They disappear.

To my left, a middle-aged man is choking on an Andrew Jackson. His arms and legs are buried. I watch him get trampled, as a crowd of money-grabbers knock him aside.

(Camera three)

Damion removes his fedora, fills it with cash.

(Camera four)

Bertha is up to her tits in cash; she's buried under a mountain of green.

"Bruce! Make it stop! No more money. Pleeeease."

Her words scatter like paper in the breeze.

(Camera one)

I shrug.

"Looks like Bertha got a bad deal!"

I'm surprised at how calm I sound. In truth, I'm petrified. She's not the only one being buried alive. One wrong move and I'm a goner.

(Camera three)

Damion soars across the stadium. The scoreboard lights up. Bertha's name flashes across the screen. Apparently, she's up by seven.

(Camera four)

Bertha is choking on cash, tears leaking from her frantic eyes.

(Split screen)

The Devil, delighted in her discomfort, applauds.

"You're rich, Bertha!"

His laughter fills the stadium, plus millions of homes in Hell, with dread.

Bertha cusses.

Damion waves his finger, giving her a no-no gesture.

(Overhead camera)

The audience is in a frenzy. A family of four are holding hands, saying prayers. They're drowning. Quickly, the children disappear. The mother shrieks, "Nooooooo!" The father frantically cries, "Someone doooo something!"

The Devil zooms across the field.

(Cut to camera five)

"Here to help," he says.

The Devil flicks his finger, and punts the parents across the field for a pair of field goals.

"Six points!" I proclaim.

Under siege, the stadium succumbs to chaos. On the jumbo screen, a teenager, with earbuds dangling from his skinny neck, is trying to escape. "The doors are locked!" Someone shoves him aside; he goes sprawling down a flight of stairs, face-first. He lands with a thud. A blonde woman wearing golden earrings steps on his back, while her partner snatches the teen's wallet. As they turn away, an avalanche buries them alive.

(Camera four)

The contestant is trying to speak, but her mouth is stuffed with cash. She's choking. Her eyes pop, as the realization hits her: She's going to die.

(Close up of contestant)

Her eyes disappear. Only her head remains. Then, she's gone.

(Camera one)

I point and shrug.

"Big Bertha forgot to read the fine print!"

I hate the sound of my voice.

(Overhead camera)

Damion races towards me, his pitchforked tail blowing in the breeze. As he approaches, a haggard-looking man, waist deep in money, swipes his ankle. Damion hoofs him into the end zone.

"It's good" I say, automatically, surprising myself. "The home team leads by two!"

(Split screen)

The audience is frantic. Audience members are jumping over railings, trying to escape. The entire field is buried alive.

Money keeps falling, there's no avoiding it; I wiggle my toes, making sure they still work.

(Camera two)

I straighten up.

There's no sign of Bertha. Only a sea of green.

"Looks like Bertha got more than she bargained for!"

(Split screen)

Damion grins menacingly at the camera.

"Yes, she most certainly did."

He's playing with his tail.

Audience members are trying to free themselves. Their efforts are in vain. The cameras, mounted on drones, capture everything.

(Close up of the Devil)

Damion regards me pitifully, then turns to the camera and winks.

"Bruce," the delight in his voice sickens me. "You're drowning!"

I am. I really am.

(Camera three)

Damion zooms over, lands on my head. Perched like a bird, he snaps his fingers. The sound is like a sonic boom. Suddenly, we're back in the studio. So is the audience, the lucky ones, that is, who've managed to stay alive.

(Split screen)

"Now," he drags the word through the mud. "What's this I hear of you wanting a salary increase?"

I gulp. This is news to me.

(Camera one)

My bald forehead gleams across the screen like a greasy burger.

The audience nervously laughs.

(Camera three)

Damion snaps his fingers. Another contract appears. He hands it to me.

My hands wobble as I give it a glance.

"Now that's what I call a raise!"

I say this involuntarily. Damion is lurking over me, hatred fuming from his unholy pores. When he touches my shoulder, I shudder.

Smoke fills the studio.

(Close up of Damion)

The Devil snickers into the camera.

"Whatcha think? Should Bruce sign?"

The audience cheers.

Damion hands me his pen, which is surprisingly heavy. His cold, calculated eyes never leaving mine.

(Camera one)

Looking nervously at the audience, I raise my arms in a vee.

"Should I sign?"

The audience chants: "SIGN IT... SIGN IT... SIGN IT....".

My eyes catch the dollar amount carved onto the paper. It's lucrative. So much so, I'd say it's too good to be true. The problem is: I'm too scared to read the fine print, although the rational part of my mind is screaming at me to do so. All the while, my pounding heart threatens to explode. Making a deal with the devil is the furthest thing from my mind.

(Split screen)

"Go on," says the Devil. "Whatcha afraid of?"

"SIGN IT… SIGN IT… SIGN IT…."

I wipe my forehead.

"Jeez. Talk about pressure."

The Devil crosses his arms.

Reluctantly, I sign.

The crowd roars its approval.

(Camera two)

"Well, there you have it folks."

Close up on me, sweating.

"Bertha got more than she'd bargained for. And apparently, I did too!"

(Cue the creepy music)

"I hope you had as much fun as we did. And I look forward to seeing you on the next episode of…"

(Cue the audience)

"LET'S MAKE A DEAL WITH THE DEVIL."

Let's Make A Deal With The Devil

Season 2 Finale:

"You look worried Bruce," my producer jokes, moments before going live. "Even for you."

This gets a chuckle from the crew.

"Quiet on the set!"

I'm already shaking in my shoes. Not a good sign. Working for the Devil is extremely stressful. And dangerous. And certainly not for the faint of heart. Why I took this gig is beyond me.

(Cue creepy music)

"Going live in five…four…three…"

I get the nod.

(Camera one)

"Greetings Hell Beings and hell raisers. Welcome to the Season 2 finale of…."

(Cue the audience)

"LET'S MAKE A DEAL WITH THE DEVIL."

I wave my arms in the air.

The audience jumps to their feet.

Someone heckles.

"Alright. Knock it off."

I serve up my best game show-host grin. It looks as fake as this cheap Hollywood studio.

"As you probably know, my name is Bruce Davie, and I'm the host of…"

(Cue audience)

"LET'S MAKE A DEAL WITH THE DEVIL."

There's a disturbance in the audience. A crew member forcefully removes someone. The commotion settles, and I get the go-ahead.

"Phew! A feisty crowd tonight!"

My painted-on smile takes up the entire screen. So does my gleaming bald head.

"Now I know what you're thinking. What's the Devil got in store for us this evening?"

The audience rumbles.

I shrug.

"Honestly, I wish I knew!"

This is true. But I'm sure it has something to do with me spending an eternity in Hell. It's right there in my contract, which runs out after this episode.

(Camera two)

"So, without further ado, let's bring out tonight's contestants, shall we?"

The audience roars.

"And yes, you heard me correctly. Tonight, for the first time ever in this show's defamatory history, we've got two contestants!"

Audience is on their feet, whooping and hollering.

(Camera three)

(Cue music)

A middle-aged couple promenade towards the podium. They're dressed like cowboys, and walk with a sense of purpose.

(Split screen)

"Welcome, both of you."

More like: Welcome to your funeral.

"Tell us a wee bit about yourselves, why don't you?"

(Camera four)

The woman speaks first. Her hair is amber, her complexion as pale as light beer.

"Well, Bruce. My name is Stacy. I'm a stay-at-home mom. This here's my partner, Tex. He owns a gun shop. We live in Austin Texas, with three beautiful children, with us here tonight."

She points.

(Overhead camera)

Two tall boys and a young girl, each dressed head-to-toe in denim, stand and bow.

The audience applauds.

(Split screen)

The other contestant approaches the microphone. He's as tall as an ivory tower, with a voice like a banjo.

"Howdy Bruce. Good to be here."

He tilts his cowboy hat. His square jaw and rugged good looks give Chuck Norris a run for his money.

I salute them.

(Camera two)

"Well then, now that we're finished with the formalities, I do believe it's time to…"

(Cue audience)

"BRING OUT THE DEVIL."

(Cue creepy music)

(Cue pyrotechnics)

The stage fills with fire and brimstone. Pentagrams slice through the air. The Devil appears suddenly, dressed in a shiny new devil suit, tailored specifically for tonight's show. It's jet-black, and leaves little to the imagination. His pitchforked tail follows closely behind him as he approaches the podium.

(Camera five)

The Devil wraps his arms around the two contestants, kisses them both on the cheek.

Tex, clearly perturbed, winces, then grudgingly wipes his cheek.

The Devil snarls, then looks him up and down, patting him down with the cup of his hand.

"Looks like everything isn't bigger in Texas," the Devil teases. Suddenly, he's grown over eight-feet tall, looming over the tall Texan.

(Camera three)

I shrug.

"What an exciting night this promises to be!"

Stacy steps forward.

"You bet it is, Bruce. We've watched every episode. We just love…"

(Cue the audience)

"LET'S MAKE A DEAL WITH THE DEVIL."

"Of course!" Damion boasts. "This is Hell's most popular show. And for good reason."

(Split screen)

He slaps the woman's backside with his tail, then raises his eyebrows mockingly. The cowboy puffs out his chest, fists clenched, daring him to touch his wife again.

"Woah, easy there pardner."

Damion nudges Tex.

Stacy is flushed. "Don't mind Tex. He's the jealous type."

"Oh really?"

Damion's tail is now shaped like a lasso. With it, he snags Stacy and pulls her close.

Her face turns tomato-red.

The cowboy grunts, pulling it off with one strong swoop.

The audience boos.

The Devil snickers.

I feel sick. If this is to be my last episode (or final day on Earth), I don't want it spoiled by this denim-clad dude whose hat is bigger than his brains; or by Damion, who seems feisty tonight. Even for him.

(Camera one)

I clear my throat.

"Tell us, Stacy and Tex…no, tell all of Hell…what it is your beating hearts desire?"

The audience is on the edge of their seats.

(Split screen)

The Texans exchange doubtful looks.

The wife takes charge.

"Well Bruce," Stacy says. "We don't want anything that might get us killed. Being from Dallas, we were raised with some common sense."

The audience hisses.

(Camera five)

The husband steps up.

"That's right, Bruce. Simply put, we want to be famous for a day. That's it. Then we can write a book and live off the royalties."

The audience erupts into a frenzy of catcalls.

(Camera three)

The Devil's eyebrows touch the top of his head. His voice slithers like a snake.

"Is that so?"

My heart plummets. These Texans are flirting with disaster. If they'd stuck to the script, they might be safe. They were supposed to ask for a lifetime's supply of Super Bowl tickets. Easy-peasy. Who do these cowpokes think they are? Do they really think they can outsmart the Devil?

"Well," I say, shakily. "I'm sure Damion can arrange that."

I raise my arms.

"What does the audience think?"

The audience goes ballistic.

(Camera four)

The Devil, still towering over the Texans, leans into the camera.

"Famous, eh?"

His lips smack against his face. When he touches the dude's shoulder, the cowboy swipes his arm away.

The audience boos. Someone tosses an egg onto the podium, narrowly missing the contestants.

"Woah! Easy does it!" I spurt out.

All hell breaks loose.

(Overhead camera)

The crew gets busy, disposing of the egg and the agitator.

(Camera one)

I wipe my sweaty forehead.

"Tough crowd."

The audience hoots.

The Devil sneers.

"SILENCE!"

Flames flash across the room.

People shriek, including me.

(Close up of Damion)

The Devil, boasting his gambler's grin, turns to the contestants.

"Yes, yes. You WILL be famous. But just for one day."

The audience roars their approval.

I shudder. Never in all my years, have I felt so much animosity from an audience. I'll be lucky to make it out alive.

(Split screen)

"Sounds like the Devil has a plan."

I try to sound cheerful. But cheerfulness is the opposite of how I feel.

(Camera one)

"Tell us Damion…and all of Hell…what you've got cooked up?"

The audience leans in.

(Camera three)

The Devil winks at Stacy.

"Well, I do believe it's time for those two cowpokes to become famous. Am I correct?"

The audience jumps to their feet, chanting: "FAMOUS…. FAMOUS…. FAMOUS…."

(Split screen)

Stacy is pleased. Her partner, on the other hand, is showing concern. His shoulders are tense, he's swallowed his bottom lip.

Damion dazzles the audience.

"Famous, y'all shall be."

He snaps his fingers.

BAM.

The studio goes dark.

Someone in the audience screams.

Stacy gasps.

Tex grunts.

(Camera one)

I shrug.

Is this Damion's latest trick? Or did they finally cut the power? We give the impression that this show is hugely popular; but in truth, outside of Hell, this show is a dud. Cable and internet companies avoid us like the plague.

(Overhead camera)

The contestants vanish under a cloud of fog.

A flaming pentagram floats across the stage.

"Well, isn't that just dandy!"

The Devil points to the large screen behind the audience.

"Mister and Missus Cowpoke are about to jump the falls!"

He snaps his fingers, then he disappears.

My legs go weak. My heart is beating irregularly again. I still don't know he does it. How any of this works. Suddenly, I'm alone on stage, shaking in my fine Italian boots, while the audience grows rowdier by the second.

Cameras mounted on drones are pointed at Tex and Stacy, who are trapped inside a large, steel barrel, with Niagara Falls looming below them.

Damion flies across the falls, lands next to Tex.

The Devil taps the barrel.

"Ain't she a beauty?"

The audience hurrahs.

The barrel is unlike anything I've ever seen. Although it's huge, and probably weighs a ton, it barely contains the two Texans, who are kicking and screaming, cursing up a storm.

"Get me the hell out of here!" Stacy's voice rips through the noise of the falls. "NOW!"

Damion frowns.

"You wanted to be famous. Am I right?"

The audience chants, "FAMOUS…. FAMOUS…. FAMOUS…."

Tex pokes his head out of the barrel, cowboy hat and all.

"Now wait one minute, Damion. That's unfair. We wanted fame. Not death."

The Devil chuckles.

"The two are synonymous, am I right?"

The audience agrees.

Damion checks his watch.

"Well then..."

He slams the lid shut.

That's the end of the Texans, as far as I'm concerned.

(Close up of Damion)

"Whatcha think? Should they jump the falls?"

The audience shouts, "JUMP…. JUMP…. JUMP…."

(Camera two)

My insides are melting. I'm petrified. You'd think working with the Devil would get easier over time. You'd be dead wrong.

"Looks like the people have spoken!" I hear myself say.

The audience continues their chant.

(Overhead camera)

"Excellent," Damion says, fiddling his fingers.

He looks over the cliff, and makes a sour face.

"Wowsers. That's a long way down!"

"JUMP…. JUMP…. JUMP…."

"And so much water!"

(Camera one)

My worried-sick face appears on the screen.

I straighten up.

"Once they jump, Tex and Stacy will surely be famous!"

Except of course, they won't be famous. Not in this world anyways. They've been duped. Why these people sign up to die is beyond me. Perhaps we've reached a spectacular level of stupidity in human evolution.

(Overhead camera)

Damion's lips stretch across his reddened face, his arms flex like a weightlifter.

"I'll give them a helping hand."

He rolls the giant barrel to the very edge of the cliff, ignoring the banging and hollering coming from within the steel coffin.

"Stacy, Tex…" His lips stretch into a snarl. "Prepare for fame!"

The audience is on their feet.

Damion shoves the barrel over the edge.

(Split screen)

The barrel tumbles down the falls, disappearing into the fast-moving water.

The audience holds its breath.

(Spy camera)

Inside the barrel, the Texans are shrieking. Their heads and arms and legs collide. Chunks of puke pour across Stacy's sickening face, who's calling Tex every name in the book, and it's a big book. Meanwhile, Tex is like a frog in a blender. His face is green, his nose is broken; blood is leaking from every orifice.

There's a loud crash as the barrel plunders underwater.

(Overhead camera)

The barrel resurfaces, traveling dangerously downstream.

The audience is back on their feet, fists-pumping.

(Split screen)

What troubles me is how the pedestrians and tourists, crowding the streets, remain oblivious. To them, this is nothing out of the ordinary. Nobody watches, or even takes a pic. I'm starting to suspect foul play. Somehow, Damion is controlling this. He's using dark magic. A spell. Maybe it's not real. But it is real.

(Camera one)

I'm trembling.

"What a jump!" my voice ricochets off the studio walls. "They'll be famous in no time!"

The audience chants:

"FAMOUS…. FAMOUS…. FAMOUS…."

(Closeup of the Devil)

"Yes, yes. An excellent jump, I must say."

He peaks over the edge.

"Looks like they could use some help."

(Cut to overhead camera)

Damion flies towards the barrel, which is bouncing off rocks and debris.

(Spy camera)

Blood. So much blood in such a tight space. Stacy's hair is in disarray. Her face is beyond repair. Tex swallowed his hat. One of his eyeballs is bouncing like a Superball. His left arm is flapping nonsensically. It isn't attached.

(Camera four)

The Devil scoops up the barrel, then flies to shore. When his feet touch the ground, he shakes off the water, cat-like, then glares at the camera.

"What a jump!"

He cranks open the lip.

(Split screen)

Stacy spills out. So does Tex's left arm.

The audience gasps.

Damion applauds.

"Such valor and swagger!"

(Camera five)

Stacy is flopping fish-like, barely clinging to life. Her mouth is full of blood and brains.

The Devil puts his foot on her head.

"SAY CHEESE."

From out of nowhere, a photographer appears.

SNAP.

Damion, looking pleased with himself, is suddenly holding a newspaper.

(Closeup of newspaper)

The headline splashes across the screen: IDIOTS JUMP THE FALLS.

(Camera four)

Damion shoves the newspaper in front of her face.

"Looks like Tex and Stacy are famous."

Stacy's eyes twitch. Clearly, she needs medical assistance. I'm surprised she's still alive; her husband's brains splattered across the inside of the barrel. The very sight making me gag.

Stacy tries to speak, but fails, her eyes filled with rage.

Damion tosses the leftover arm into the water, then shrugs.

"Sorry about your hubby."

(Camera two)

With wobbly knees, I face the audience.

"Looks like the barrel got the best of Tex!"

The audience bellows.

I continue to talk involuntarily.

"Gosh dolly. Look at all that blood!"

"MORE BLOOD… MORE BLOOD… MORE BLOOD…."

I find myself chanting along.

Suddenly, my vision blurs. I clutch my chest. Maybe I'll suffer a heart attack on live TV. Hell waits for no one, I suppose.

(Camera four)

Stacy spits blood on Damion's boot.

"Devil be damned." I blurt.

Damion's face twists into a ball of fury.

"Now, now, Stacy. That wasn't very nice."

He crushes her fingers with his boots.

Stacy yelps.

"I was gonna save your long-limbed partner over there," he points. "Not anymore!"

The audience is bloodthirsty. Paper airplanes and rotten eggs whizz past me. I duck just in time.

(Closeup of contestant)

Stacy's tongue is leaking from her bloodied face. She's missing her front teeth. Damion digs his spiky heel deep into her blood-soaked abdomen.

"I reckon you'll need medical assistance."

He snaps his fingers.

Suddenly, they're back in the studio.

Damion is as happy as a filthy pig. Next to him is Stacy, who's caked in blood and gore. Her corpse-of-a-husband spills from the gigantic steel barrel, taking center stage.

(Overhead camera)

The contestant's children rush the stage. They're delirious.

The crew hurry out and drag them aside, along with Stacy, who's rushed to the hospital, where she will certainly die.

"Now that's what I call speedy service!"

My voice appalls me. So does this job. If only I'd listened to my mother, and got into politics.

Damion snaps his finger, then disappears under a plume of dusty smoke.

(Camera one)

"Well, there you have it folks. That's the last you'll see of Tex and Stacy. But fret not, they had their moment of fame…in Hell!"

The audience is tossing trash onto the stage.

I narrowly dodge a projectile.

"Hope you've enjoyed Season Two as much as I did."

I hated it.

"And, unless the Devil strikes me down," and he very-well might, "I hope to see you this Fall, for Season Three of…"

(Cue the audience)

"LET'S MAKE A DEAL WITH THE DEVIL."

Let's Make A Deal With The Devil!
Season 3 Premiere:

"Hard to believe you've lasted this long!" one of the camera operators jokes.

I gulp. The previous host lasted three episodes. Now, he's dead.

"Ready Bruce?" the producers shouts, not waiting for a response.

The lights dim, the audience shuffles in their seats.

My worried face splatters across the monitor.

Smoke fills the studio.

(Enter Music)

(Camera one)

We're live.

"Howdy doody hobgoblins and hooligans!" I wipe my forehead, "Phew! What a long strange trip it's been!"

The audience shuffles in their seats.

"My name's Bruce Davies, the longest-lasting host of…"

(Cue the audience)

"LET'S MAKE A DEAL WITH THE DEVIL."

(Overhead camera)

It's Devil's Night; the audience consists of ghosts and goblins and creepy-looking creatures. The clarity of their costumes troubles me. Then again, they're probably not costumes.

(Camera one)

"Alrighty then. What do you say? Should we bring out tonight's contestant?"

The audience shrugs.

I yank my collar, comically.

"Lemme repeat the question, for those of you at the back: Should we bring out tonight's contestant?"

(Cue audience)

Audience applauds.

"Now, that's more like it."

(Cue creepy music)

(Camera four)

A hulk of a man, clad in a bazaar superhero costume, races across the stage, flapping his arms like a bird. His muscles ripple as he moves.

The audience roars.

The contestant, boasting a pallet of sparkling teeth, is covered head-to-toe in tight-fitting spandex. His cape is banana-yellow, the rest of him is orange. There's a sinister-looking logo on his chest, V-shaped, with a bloodied eyeball in the middle.

(Camera two)

I point my thumb. "Yikes. Wouldn't wanna meet this fella in a back alley, if ya know what I mean?"

The audience boos.

"Alright, alright. Knock it off!"

(Split screen)

I turn to the contestant. "Tell us about yourself. Starting with that strange costume you're wearing."

(Camera five)

The contestant lowers himself to reach the microphone.

"Well, Bruce, my name's Tyrone Jackson. I'm from Jersey City. And I'm here to kick some ass. Hell yeah!"

The audience jumps to their feet, cheering.

There's a ruckus in the back. Security rushes over; someone is ejected.

I sigh. Things are falling apart. On live television, no less. Good thing no one on Earth watches this show, aside from the hapless few who sign up to die.

"W-well then," I stutter. "We'll see about that."

(Camera one)

I straighten my tie. "Alrighty. I do believe it's time to…"

(Cue audience)

"BRING OUT THE DEVIL."

(Cue creepy music)

Flames flash across the ominous stage.

The audience ahs.

Damion appears; he's wearing his classic red leather devil suit and impossibly dark sunglasses.

(Split screen)

Tyrone is standing broad-chested.

Damion regards the large specimen standing before him with contempt. "Here." He tosses the contestant his sunglasses, who fumbles them in surprise.

"Whoopsies," Damion snickers. "A wee bit jumpy, eh?"

The contestant growls.

"No sir." Tyrone grunts. He crushes the sunglasses with one hand, then he steps on them.

The audience gasps.

(Camera two)

Cautiously, I face the contestant.

"Um, now that we know each other a little bit better, why don't you tell the Devil what your heart desires?"

(Camera four)

The broad-shouldered contestant licks his face, leans into the mic. "Bruce," he says with a simper, "I'm here to steal your job."

The audience jumps to their feet, chanting. "STEAL YOUR JOB…. STEAL YOUR JOB…."

(Split screen)

Unknowingly, I clutch my chest. My heart is thumping irregularly again. Meanwhile, the audience continues chanting: "STEAL YOUR JOB…. STEAL YOUR JOB…."

Damion is enraged, eyes like fireballs.

"SILENCE!"

The audience obeys.

(Close up of the Devil)

Damion smirks, fidgeting. "Now, that's more like it."

His voice slithers down my spine like warm soup.

(Split screen)

Damion, looking sharply at the contestant, snaps his fingers. A contract appears. He hands it to Tyrone, who's shaking his head.

The audience leans in.

"Damion," the contestant says, as if talking to a child, "We don't need no contract."

He tears it into tiny pieces.

"Holy hell!" I blurt.

Damion is stunned, but only for a second, then he composes himself.

"Well then," Damion's voice drops an octave, which I believe to be his true voice. "What do you have in mind?"

The audience is dead silent.

(Camera three)

The contestant rubs his hands. "A contest, plain and simple."

(Camera two).

"A contest?" my voice squeaks.

I regard the audience.

"Whatcha think? Should Tyrone get his contest?"

"CONTEST…. CONTEST…. CONTEST…."

(Overhead camera)

Damion is seething.

"Well then," I say shakily, "The audience has spoken."

The audience cheers.

(Camera two)

"But," I interrupt, "You know the rules, right?"

(Cue the audience)

"THE DEVIL'S IN THE DETAILS."

(Camera three)

Damion wags his tail, grins coyly.

"Yes," he says slowly, looking directly at me. "We shall have a contest."

I'm the sacrificial lamb. His eyes tell me so.

Damion laughs; then using his tail, he spanks the contestant.

Tyrone grunts, then throws the Devil across the stage.

The audience hisses, throwing eggs and rotten tomatoes.

The stage hand cleans up the mess.

(Camera two)

My pale face reappears on the monitors.

"Well, ain't that the Devil incarnate?"

"Shut up, Bruce." Damion snaps. Suddenly, he's nine feet tall, and towering over the contestant. "You… ever… touch… me… again…"

He digs his bony finger deep into the contestant's well-chiselled chest.

All at once, the studio walls disappear. Suddenly, we're hovering high above a volcano. The heat is face-melting. As I get a better view, my stomach sinks. That's not a volcano down there. It's Hell. The screams of the dead prove this to be true.

Cameras mounted on drones whizz by in a blur, capturing everything.

Damion's eyes are glowing.

"Well then," he snarls. "Let's get on with it, shall we?"

He snaps his finger.

Two old-fashioned school desks appear, facing each other, with a chair on each end. Damion points to the chairs.

"Sit."

I sit.

He regards the contestant with malice. "Go on, then."

Reluctantly, the contestant sits, which isn't easy. The chair barely contains his extraordinary girth.

Face to face, with only a small desk separating us, Tyrone and I exchange doubtful looks. He's gonna make mincemeat out of me. I know this, Tyrone does too.

"Your job is mine," he mutters through clenched teeth.

I shiver.

Damion is dressed as a referee, wetting the whistle in his mouth.

"The contest is simple," he says. "Arm wrestle. Best two out of three."

The audience erupts.

Damion hovers over us. "Lock hands."

My hand disappears inside Tyrone's ginormous mitt. He squeezes; the pain is egregious.

"I'm left-handed," he declares. "But that shouldn't be a problem."

The audience leans in.

"Who's ready to rumble?" Damion asks the bloodthirsty audience.

The audience goes ballistic.

"Now wait a minute!" I try in vain to free my hand.

Damion places his cold, clammy hands over ours.

"Aaaaad GO!"

He blows the whistle.

With one quick swoop Tyrone snaps my arm like a twig.

The audience boos.

I cry in agony. My shoulder is broken. My hand hurts like hell. Clearly, I need medical attention.

"The contestant is up by one," Damion says.

Tyrone flexes his muscles to the adoring audience. "You're next, Damion."

The devil licks his lips, then he places a hand on my shoulder. Immediately, a surge of supernatural strength arrives.

"You okay Bruce?" the Devil teases. "You're not going to lose your job, on live television no less, to this despicable dingbat, are you?"

I can't tell if he's being ironic, or just plain mean. Probably both.

Damion isn't finished.

"Not to sound offensive, but…" He flaps the contestant's cape. "Whatcha supposed to be anyway? Captain Steroid?"

The audience chuckles.

Tyrone tries to crush my hand; but with my new-found strength, he cannot. I squeeze back, mightily.

"Aaaaand GO!"

Damion blows the whistle.

(Split screen)

The audience is chanting, but I don't make out what they're saying. I'm busy fighting for my job. And my life. Grunting and groaning, I edge the contestant's arm toward the desk; but he's stubborn, refusing to give up. Our arms are locked. Back and forth we go. Sweat stings my eyes. I panic. He's overpowering me. The hairs on my hand brush the desk, my arm is bending in all the wrong places. My grip tightens. Muscles explode from my biceps. With every ounce of strength I have, I force his hand to the desk.

The audience boos.

(Camera three)

"Would ya look at that!" Damion gloats. "Didn't see THAT coming!"

Tyrone is glaring at me; he knows I'm cheating. In a flash, he leaps to his feet, but Damion forces him to sit.

"Going somewhere, Captain Steroid?"

Tyrone is about to speak, but thinks better of it.

"This is it," Damion declares. "The final countdown."

He snaps his fingers.

From out of nowhere, the Final Countdown soars, catchy keyboard riffs and all, sending a surge of adrenaline my way. Damion puts my hand into the contestant's.

"Now wait one minute!" the contestant cries. He offers his left hand. "Fair is fair." He winks.

Damion shrugs.

"Goooooo!"

The sound of the whistle sends us off.

(Split screen)

Tyrone's grip is unyielding, as he forces my arm backwards. But I resist; veins explode from my neck, as my left arm bends unnaturally. Back and forth we go. I'm about to give in, when another surge of strength arrives like cavalry.

I grit my teeth. "Oh no you don't."

All my knuckles crack at once.

Tyrone scoffs. "Give up, Bruce. Your days are numbered."

He forces my arm dangerously close to the desk. Feet flailing, I'm trying every trick I know. But it's no use. Nothing works. I'm losing.

My foot finds a latch.

"What the?"

Then it hits me, clear as a summer sky: This is all an illusion. Trickery coming from Damion's sadistic and twisted mind. We're still inside the cheap Hollywood studio. None of this is real!

Tyrone is a dog, foam frothing from his tightly-masked face. "You're going down, Bruce!"

He applies more pressure; everything he has.

My eyes are bulging from their sockets. I can't take much more of this. With my foot hovering over the latch, I pull the lever. Then, SWOOSH.

"See you in Hell, Captain Steroid."

All at once, the ground opens up, and the contestant disappears into the flames of Hell. A furious flash of lightning zips across the sky.

Then suddenly, we're back inside the studio, and I'm on my feet, staring into the lens of a camera, clutching my chest.

(Split screen)

Damion sneaks me a sinister smirk.

"Excellent work Bruce. Cunning and creative."

I shrug, trying to catch my breath.

"I hope we've all learned a valuable lesson tonight."

Damion raises his arms to the adorning audience.

"THE DEVIL GETS HIS DUE."

"Well, that's enough fun for one evening." Damion tips his non-existent hat, then disappears under a cloud of thick smoke, leaving me to fend for myself.

(Camera one)

"That's the last we'll see of Tyrone. Unless of course he makes it into a Marvel movie."

Rotten eggs pummel the stage.

"Well, I hope you had as much fun as I did."

I wipe egg from my face.

"I hope to see you next week for another exciting addition of…"

(Cue the audience)

"LET'S MAKE A DEAL WITH THE DEVIL."

Let's Make A Deal With The Devil!
Season 3: FINALE:

"Quiet on the set!"

My worried face splashes across the monitors. Geesh. Am I really that old?

"Aaaaaand, we're live!"

(Camera one)

I suck in my gut.

"Greetings! My name is Bruce Davie, and I'm the host of…"

(Cue the Audience)

"LET'S MAKE A DEAL WITH THE DEVIL."

(Camera two)

"Gosh darnit folks, we've done it. We've reached the end of yet another season. Who woulda thunk it?"

Someone in the audience shouts, "You suck, Bruce!"

I tip my non-existing hat.

"Yes, I do have something in common with your mother."

The audience boos. Profanities drop like bombs.

"Anywho, we've got a special show planned for tonight." I pause for suspense. "After scouring the galaxy far and wide, searching for the perfect guest…"

The audience leans in.

"Please put your hands together for tonight's guest, hailing from the land of moose and hockey sticks."

(Cue Canadian anthem)

A dill pickle-of-a-man with unkempt hair and watery eyes approaches the podium. He's wearing a lumberjack sweater and jeans so old, it's impossible to tell their true color.

(Camera three)

Clearly, he's drunk. His words soar like hockey pucks.

"Thanks Bruce. Good t' be here. Watched all yer episodes. Yessir. Including da one where yer pants fell down. Saw yer little wiener too, I did!"

The audience is stunned.

(Camera two)

I shrug, not having understood one word the man said, except the wiener bit, but I digress.

"Alrighty then. Let's start with your name, and where you're from? Can you do that?"

(Split screen)

The contestant nods politely.

"Yes boi. M' names Pete. Pete Tailor. From St. John's Newfoundland, I am. Whattaya at?"

The audience is scratching their heads. I don't blame them. The man's accent is thicker than a ten-pound moose steak.

"Woah, simmer down, partner."

The contestant chuckles.

"Oh sure. Ye Yanks are a bit slow between the ears, eh?"

He winks.

The audience boos. More F-bombs are dropped.

(Split screen)

My jaw falls to my feet. I'm dumbfounded. The last thing I want to do is screw up the season finale. Again.

"Um, let's bring out the Devil, shall we?"

(Cue creepy music)

The lights dim.

A fiery pentagram floats across the stage, then – POOF – the Devil appears out of thin air. He's dressed in a tuxedo-style devil suite with fancy red stitching, and shiny black boots.

The audience jumps to their feet.

Damion salutes.

"Good evening. How's everyone doing tonight?"

The audience hoots and hollers.

"Excellent." Damion turns to the contestant, regarding him with disdain. "A Newfie, huh?"

(Overhead camera)

The contestant looks him up and down.

"Yer some nasty, wha? Where'd ya get that suit? Walmart?"

The audience chuckles.

Damion sneers.

I bite my bottom lip.

The contestant stands on his tip toes.

"How's da view up there?"

Damion growls; flames flash from his furious eyes.

The audience gasps.

"Alrighty then," I intervene. "Pete, please tell the Devil why you're here."

In truth, he's here because no one in the USA signed up. Literally, Pete's the bottom of the barrel.

(Camera four)

The contestant rolls up his sleeves, revealing a tattoo of a lobster swimming in a sea of freckles.

"Oh, sure," he says languidly. "I ran outta Newfie Juice."

The audience is gobsmacked.

(Split screen)

I do a double-take.

"Excuse me?"

Pete huffs.

"Wha? Hard of hearing, are ya?"

The audience roars.

Damion shouts at the director, "For the love of Satan, can we get a translator?"

Pete makes a coo-coo gesture, says, "Not too bright, eh?"

My anxiety is skyrocketing. Trouble is brewing, and I'm smack dab in the middle.

Damion's voice drops an octave.

"Listen here, you little twerp. Show some respect, or I'll cut off your head and stuff it down your throat! Capeesh?"

The ground trembles as he speaks, the lights flicker, and a sense of doom wafts over the studio. I trip into camera one, breaking the lens in the process. The camera person swears, before disappearing backstage in a fit of rage.

"Whoopsies!" the contestant blurts.

(Camera two)

I straighten up.

"Pete, you'd better repeat yourself. What is it you truly desire? But please, speak slowly."

(Camera four)

The contestant makes a chugging gesture. "Screech," he says. "Powerful stuff. Puts hair on yer chest, yessir!"

The audience cheers.

(Split screen)

The devil snarls.

"Liquor? Are you telling me you want…liquor?"

"Aye."

"Whatever ales ya!" I exclaim.

"Shut up, Bruce!" Damion forks his tongue. "Yes, yes. You shall have your liquor. Your…Newfie Juice!"

He snaps his fingers.

Boxes of Screech appear next to Pete, who's wide-eyed and visibly excited.

"Dat's more like it!"

He reaches for a box.

"HALT!"

Everything stops. Nobody breathes. You can hear a pin drop.

"First, you must sign the contract. I can't just GIVE you the damned Screech, can I?"

Damion produces a contract made of human skin.

Pete shakes his head.

"Nah. In Newfoundland, a good ol' handshake will do ya."

Damion grimaces.

"Fine. Have it your way."

They shake hands for an uncomfortable length of time. Pete fails at overpowering Damion; instead, he's sent flying across the room, crashing into a stack of boxes.

Grinning coyly, Damion flexes his muscles, and does an evil dance, while the audience cheers him on: "SATAN…. SATAN…. SATAN…"

Meanwhile, Pete opens a bottle of Screech and takes a swallow. He returns to the podium, bottle in hand, and offers the devil a drink.

(Camera two)

I groan.

"What does the audience think? Should the devil have a drink?"

(Overhead camera)

"DRINK…. DRINK…. DRINK…. DRINK…"

I nod approvingly.

"The people have spoken!"

I've trained myself not to look scared. But in truth, I'm petrified. Things are about to get ugly. And fast. Only fools drink with the devil.

(Camera three)

"DRINK…. DRINK…. DRINK…"

The Devil blushes.

"Well, twist my evil arm."

The Devil snaps his fingers.

Suddenly, we're in a seedy nightclub, wreaking of urine. The room is dimly lit and lined with human skulls. Plumes of smoke sift languidly through the stale air, like polluted clouds. We're cramped inside a booth; an unopened bottle of Screech, plus three shot glasses, greet us.

The bartender arrives: a vampire, with long fangs protruding from his ashen face. He's tall, thin and shockingly handsome.

"Damion!" he hisses. "How wonderful to see you! It's been…too long."

Damion groans.

"Hello Sergio."

The bartender wipes the blood off the table, drops an ashtray, then scampers away.

Pete opens the bottle of rum, pours three tall shots. Then his eyes meet mine.

"C'mon Bruce, have a grog!"

Nervously, I step out of the booth. The floor is wet and sticky and gross.

"Sorry," I say sheepishly, "I'm on the job."

Pete's disappointment is obvious.

"Suit yerself."

He hands Damion a shot. They cheers, then down the liquor.

"Ugh!" Damion spits fire, narrowly missing Pete, who's pouring more shots. They drink. The Devil grimaces. "Bloody hell!"

The bartender is watching from a distance, terrified. This worries me. Have you ever seen a scared vampire? Trust me, you don't want to. Sergio returns with a jar of insects. "Snacks," he says, joylessly, before scurrying back behind the bar.

All at once, the patrons – vampires as far as I can tell – vacate the premises. The bar empties, leaving only the three of us, plus the bartender, who's as pale as light beer.

Damion is standing on the topsy table.

"Sergio!" he slurs. "Drinks are on me!"

He snaps his fingers. The audience appears, filling the vacant booths. Bottles of Screech are passed around freely.

Pete, clearly enthralled, joins Damion on the table. "Now yer gettin' it!" he says, pouring Damion another shot.

"CHEERS."

Everyone drinks. I look away, noticing several cameras hidden in the cracks of the walls. I sigh. How the cameras can follow us is a secret I'll never know.

Damion belches; Pete matches it; and thus, a belching competition unfolds.

I'm trembling, having never seen such reckless behavior from Damion. And that's saying a lot. If he keeps this up, all Hell will break loose.

I'm about to interject, when the entrance door dings. All eyes turn. A She Devil enters, with long legs, swinging hips, and gargantuan breasts. She's wearing a necklace made of human skulls, and nothing else. Her tail swaggers, as she strolls catlike toward the Devil's booth.

"Woo we!" Damion catcalls, as She-Devil puts her arms around him. Their tongues intertwine in a grotesque display of affection. His erection is impossible to ignore.

"Well, I've seen enough!" I blurt.

Meanwhile, the audience is getting belligerent, downing rum like sailors on leave.

Pete hands me a shot.

The audience turns on me: "DRINK…. DRINK…. DRINK…. DRINK…"

Grudgingly, I oblige. "Oh good God!" The rum tastes like turpentine.

The Devil grunts as She-Devil whispers naughtily into his ear, stroking his tail. His erection knocks the table, spilling a bottle of booze.

Pete points a stubby thumb; "Whoopsie. Someone can't handle their alcohol!"

The audience snickers.

Damion turns to Pete, eyes ablaze; "You think yer hot stuff, do ya?" He grabs Pete by the collar, then knocks him flat on his ass. "You're a loser! Same goes for the rest of you!"

Pandemonium ensues. Bottles bounce across the bar in glass-shattering, rum-fueled frenzy. As I try to escape, Damion grabs the scruff of my neck.

"Going somewhere, Bruce?"

"I…I" My flailing heart is threatening to explode.

Damion sneers; "Time to teach you a lesson, once and for all."

Damion wraps his ropy fingers around my throat. I gasp for air, but my efforts are in vain. My poor excuse of a life flashes before my eyes. Everything goes grey. I'm about to die. My body goes limp.

"Shoulda done this long ago," he says, in a faraway voice.

Something crashes. My body jolts, as I tumble onto the rum-soaked floor.

Damion is shrieking; his head leaking blood; a broken bottle lay at his feet. Damion grabs the nearest audience member, snaps their neck. A fresh corpse falls over me.

"Who's next?" Damion sneers.

Someone shouts, "You suck, Damion! You're a fake!"

"Is that so?"

All at once, Damion goes on a killing spree, slaughtering the entire audience. Necks snap like turkey wishbones. Bodies drop like flies. Thick, crimson blood oozes everywhere.

A large man wearing a dress tries to stop him; Damion knocks his head clean off. The head rolls next to me, eyes open.

I gag.

Finally, the screaming stops. All that remains are headless corpses and buckets of blood, pooling across the barroom floor. The smell is vomitous.

Damion regards the gore with glee.

I step forward. "Now that's what I call clearing the bar!"

Damion snarls, reaching for my throat, looking to finish me off. Beside us, Pete cracks open a fresh bottle.

"I reckon the Devil needs a drink. Yessir."

Damion's eyes light up.

Pete pours two shots. Damion downs the shot, then suffers through another coughing fit. Pete pours three more, offering me one, to which I refuse.

Damion is enraged; "You cheap, no good, son-of-a…" As he speaks, flames flash across the barroom. The rum-soaked booth catches fire, and quickly spreads. Within seconds the entire bar is ablaze.

"Noooo!" Sergio steps out from behind the bar and rushes over, yielding a butcher's knife; the blade is long and silver and sharp. "You've been a thorn in my side for far too long!"

"Hosh posh," Damion croaks, shoving the bartender aside.

She-Devil, whose eyes dance like shooting stars, is speaking in an unknown language. Damion, clearly entranced, fails to notice Sergio sneaking up on him.

"Devil be gone!" Sergio proclaims. And with deadly precision, he slashes Damion's throat, releasing an ocean of black blood.

"NOOOOOOOOooooooo…."

Damion drops to his knees, his face twists with terror and surprise. She-Devil joins Sergio; together, they stab Damion repeatedly, spilling his guts like spaghetti. The sound is sickening. Again and again they stab, gutting him like a pig. Flames flicker from Damion's eyes, before growing dim. He collapses. The ground shakes as he falls.

Sergio stands over the Devil, knife gleaming. With She Devil by his side, he places the sharp edge of the knife against the Devil's bloodied throat. With hate-filled eyes, and with one strong swoop, Damion is decapitated. His head rolls onto the fire-riddled floor, catches fire, then explodes. The body quickly turns to acid, before dissolving into goop.

With much effort, I refrain from commenting. Words escape me. Meanwhile, the barroom continues to burn, cooking fresh corpses like Thanksgiving dinner. The smell is abhorrent. Sergio and She-Devil share a mouth-watering kiss that lasts forever.

A bomb detonates.

The world fades to black, as my body disappears. This is it. My time has come. The Lord of Death has arrived. I hear a voice. It's close. When I open my eyes, I'm standing next to Pete inside the cheap Hollywood studio. The lights are off. The power is cut. The crew is nowhere to be found. With a glimmer in his eyes, Pete offers me a bottle.

"Ah, what the hell?" I take a swallow.

Pete slaps my back.

"Yer alright, Bruce."

He saunters to the exit, carrying a box of booze. He waves goodbye and steps outside. The door slams shut behind him.

I breathe deeply, trying to calm my nerves. What the Hell just happened? Is Damion dead? Am I unemployed? So many questions. So few answers. With shaky movements, I turn to the lifeless camera, and straighten my tie.

"Pete may be going to Hell in a bucket, but at least he's enjoying the ride! And Damion, well, something tells me he's suffering from one Hell of a hangover!"

I dry my water bucket eyes. Doing my best Bob Barker impression, I sign off one last time:

"This is it, folks. We've reached the end. I hope you survived the final edition of…

Let's Make a Deal with the Devil."

Grandma's Basement

Grandma's basement was OFF LIMITS. I should never have gone down there. But I did. And I've regretted it ever since.

I was nine-years-old when it happened. My father, forced to work night overtime, dropped me off at Grandma's for the night. I cried and cried, pleading not to be left alone with her. After much fuss, Dad promised he'd try and pick me up later, but only if he finished work early. His eyes were doubtful, and didn't sooth me one bit.

Grandma had the Devil's temper. Mean as a junkyard dog, she was. And twice as ugly. Her crinkly skin clung tightly to brittle bones, but her eyes never wavered. They'd cut you down to size in an instant. That and her voice, which sounded like as dirty as an ashtray.

"Go fetch my walker!" she ordered from her spot on the couch, the moment I arrived. "And a cold root beer from the fridge while yer at it!"

I did.

When I returned, she was snoring; drops of drool decorated her furrowed face. I didn't want to disturb her – I wouldn't dare – so I left the walker leaning against the couch, and placed the root beer on the coffee table, next to the remote control.

Her home was stuffy and dungeon-dark, with boxes of junk lining the flowery walls, like ivory towers. There was nothing to do. I didn't have a cell phone or iPad, and her computer was ancient. There was only one TV, and it was so loud my ears were bleeding. My grandmother had no pets, nor friends to speak of. Ugh. Even her food sucked. I didn't know what to do, so I changed the channel.

BIG mistake.

"How dare you?" she snapped like a crocodile. "I was watching CNN."

She wasn't. But I wasn't about to mention this. Soon Grandma was snoring again. I was too scared to change the channel, so I went about searching for stuff to play with. My search was in vain. I was so bored it hurt. And only a half hour had passed. Ugh. I had to do something. Anything. There was only one place I could think of. The one place left unexplored: Grandma's Basement.

But I'd been warned:

Never.

Go.

Down.

There.

PERIOD.

But what choice did I have? Besides, I was young and naive. Being carved up and killed was way beyond my comprehension. Nine-year-olds don't get murdered by their grandmothers. Even in horror movies, they don't.

The door creaked open, seemingly on its own. I tip-toed towards the edge of the stairs and peered down. I couldn't see the bottom, but something was down there. Somehow, I knew this. I imagined the worst: snakes and spiders and ghosts and things. My tummy tightened. There was no way I was going down there. No way. Not happening. I told myself this, but I didn't listen.

I wish I had.

Slowly, I descended the rickety stairs, near-certain something would jump out. Something did: a rat. The creepy critter crawled across my foot, before scurrying into the growing darkness. I stifled a scream, then frantically found a light switch, which was coated in cobwebs.

The light was pale and narrow. Strange shadows danced along the drab and dreary walls, like ghoulish marionettes. Suddenly, I was terrified. And no wonder. I could barely see my own hand in front of my face, let alone whatever evil was lurking down there. Still, I crept onward, gripping the handrail as though my life depended on it.

There was noise. The sound was explosive. I froze. My mind going into overdrive. I feared the worst: Grandma was standing at the top of the stairs, smiling with bad intentions. I turned to check. She wasn't. Phew. With each descending step, the basement smelled worse, like moldy mushrooms. I gagged. Who could stand such a smell? The feeling of being watched grew stronger with each step. Finally, I reached the bottom of the stairs.

"Turn around," a tiny voice warned me. "NOW."

The voice was correct. My nine-year-old self was petrified. I turned, ready to charge upstairs. The door slammed shut. I gulped. For a moment, time stood still. The air was moist and thick. A bad taste was forming in my mouth. The idea that I was trapped in Grandma's basement was gnawing at me. Still, I soldered on. It's just a basement, I told myself. How bad can it be?

I was searching for another light switch, when I came upon a stack of old boxes. After peeling away a layer of dusty cobwebs, I tore open the boxes. Sigh. Nothing but appliances, expired TV Guides and old 45's. With my hopes of finding long lost treasure obliterated, I decided to get my butt back upstairs, before Grandma noticed I was missing.

I was edging towards the stairs, careful not to step on anything, when something caught my eye: a treasure chest! It was big and battered, with black clasps and faded red trimming running along its sides. In its center was a large, gold lock, begging to be opened.

As I got closer, the stench intensified. Clearly, this was where the smell was coming from. With my mouth under my shirt, I wrapped my eager hands around the large lock and gave it a tug. It wouldn't budge. Not to be deterred, I kicked the lock with the heel of my foot, as hard as I could.

It worked! The chest popped open. As the dust settled, horror stole my heart. My mind bent in all the wrong places. This made no sense. No sense at all. Must be fake. But there it was, staring me in the face:

Human fingers. Wormy and shriveled and gross. Some had fingernails attached, blackened and bent; others were bloodied stumps. I rubbed my eyes, praying this was a hoax.

It wasn't.

Worse, the fingers were stuffed inside human skulls, nesting upon a bed of brittle bones. I counted twenty human skulls, maybe more. One skull in particular stole my attention. The skull was well-preserved, and filled with fresh human fingers, one of which wore a wedding ring.

Unadulterated horror descended upon me, followed by sadness. You see, my mother disappeared the previous summer. She'd been delivering winter supplies to Grandma, when she vanished – POOF – just like that. Apparently, she never made it to Grandma's. It was believed she simply packed up and left. Never to be seen again.

I stared at the freshest skull, the one with the wedding ring, and winced. Was that my mother? My heart fell to the floor. My eyes swelled with tears. Then the unthinkable happened:

"Johnny? Come quick!"

Grandma!

My heart leapt inside my throat. I nearly choked. Then without thinking, I darted upstairs, frantically trying to open the door. The door wouldn't budge. With all my might, I kicked and clawed, pulled and prodded.

"Johnny?" Grandma's voice quivered, "Come quick. I'm hungry!"

I took a deep breath, and tried again.

Nothing.

Without warning, the light flicked off; a deep darkness fell upon me. Then a terrible thought arrived: I forgot to close the treasure chest. She'll know!

"Johnny!"

Too late now. I cranked the door handle with everything I had.

CLICK.

It opened!

When I returned to the living room, Grandma was yielding a razor-sharp knife. Her eyes were oceans of murder.

"You shouldn't have gone down there, Johnny."

"I-I" I tried to say something, anything, but failed.

"What in God's green earth am I to do with you?"

Using the switchblade knife, she patted the seat next to her on the chesterfield. I couldn't resist. Her eyes were tractor beams, pulling me closer. The moment I sat down, her icy fingers roped around my wrist. She inched closer; the knife kissing my throat.

"Don't move."

With alarming speed, she produced a roll of duct tape from the closet.

"This will only hurt for a minute."

I regarded the steely knife, and gulped. My heart was pounding through my tee-shirt. I didn't want to die. Not like this. No way. But I didn't dare budge. Grandma rolled up her sleeves, then cut a long piece of tape. Her eyes never left mine. She sat next to me, clutching both knife and tape.

"It should never have come to this, Johnny. But…"

Just then, headlights splashed across the drapes, and a car pulled into the driveway.

"Daddy!"

My grandmother winced, but the knife never wavered.

Pushing her aside, I leapt from the couch and rushed outside, greeting my dad with open arms. He poked his head inside and said goodbye. Grandma smiled politely, but her eyes were ablaze. The knife and tape disappeared. Daddy and Grandma said their goodbyes, then finally we left.

On the way home, I asked my father about Mom. He ruffled my hair, then talked about the day they'd met. A story I'll never get sick of hearing. His voice quivered as he spoke. I wanted to bring up Grandma – her box of fingers and skulls, her knife and tape – but I didn't. Something in her eyes warned me not to.

...

Grandma died later that year. Good riddance. Father cleared the house, before selling it. No one was allowed to help. No funeral was held, and Father never spoke of Grandma again. Ever. In time, life went back to normal, whatever that means, and Grandma's basement became a distant memory. Except of course, in my dreams, where her basement still haunts me, even as an adult.

I moved to the west coast, and only spoke to father on holidays. That's how life goes, I suppose. Last month, my father died. Cancer got the best of him. When I cleared out his home, I stumbled upon something peculiar: Mother's wedding dress.

That's not all.

Wrapped inside were some items of interest: a human skull, human fingers, and a wedding ring.

He *knew*.

Tracy's Paintings

Tracy doesn't hate people on purpose. She's not like that. It's her paintings. They hate people. I remember her very first one, when she was still a kid. She painted a scantily clad woman sitting cross-legged in a field of fresh grass, a cluster of threatening clouds looming overhead; her auburn hair blowing wistfully in the breeze, as she gazes across the minty meadow stretching across the languid landscape.

I was shocked. Hell, I could barely scribble a stick person, let alone a full-sized painting with blended colours, depth and ingenuity. No one knew how she did it.

Tracy hung the painting in the hallway next to my bedroom. That night, haunted howls whispered into unwilling ears, as I tried to sleep.

"Hey Joey," Tracy's painting said, surly. "Get dead."

My mouth went dry, my heart beating like a hammer, as I lay trembling in the dark. The painting talked all night, calling me every name in the book. Night after sleepless night, the painting ridiculed me. After weeks of its torturous taunting, I'd had enough. Tracy's painting was ruining my life. The fact that no one believed me made it worse.

Time for revenge.

I gathered a jar of spiders. My plan was to release the creepy crawlers under her bedsheets. Tracy hates spiders. Always has. Like a thief in the night, I crept towards her bedroom. As I passed Tracy's painting, it was making weird noises. Cautiously, I entered her bedroom. Something took me by surprise: a shadow creature.

I dropped the jar and ran.

Those pesky spiders crawled into every crevasse of her bedroom. One spider – a big one with long, hairy legs and beady eyes – managed to sneak into her gym bag and lay eggs. During gym class a cluster of spiders crawled out, scaring everyone, especially my sister. Pandemonium ensued.

Tracy's painting was unimpressed. Any time I got near, it hissed. Each night, it moaned. The damned painting was relentless in its cruelty. Over time, my grades started slipping, and people were looking at me funny.

Finally, I snapped. After dark, in panic-fueled rage, I ripped the painting off the wall and beat it to death with a hammer, tossing its colorful carcass into the garbage.

"That outta do it."

It didn't.

Tracy's painting came back.

"Hey, Joey," it spat, the very next morning. "Get dead."

The painting persisted.

"You're a loser," it teased. "Nobody likes you."

When I told my parents, they scolded me for being jealous of my kid sister's talent. Whenever I confided in my friends, they'd laugh. I was all alone.

Later that summer my baseball team was looking to win the championship. It was the night before the Big Game. I was starting pitcher. The damned painting wouldn't shut up. It kept chattering away, like a drunk uncle on Super Bowl Sunday.

"Psst. Joey. You awake?"

My eyes snapped open; I gasped. A shadow creature was hovering over my bed, seething. Its eyes were black holes, digging into my soul; its shape, long and sinister, like a vampire.

"Your team sucks," it proclaimed. "You're going to lose. And everyone will blame you."

And that's exactly what happened. My team did suck, we lost the game, and everyone blamed me, including my parents. It was the worst day of my life.

Tracy spent all summer alone in her room, painting. My parents awarded her the finest of paints. By fall, when she showed me her latest piece, I nearly died:

A silver-laced city, overtly modern, yet somehow rundown, crowded over a street of tattoos; a spec of pale light trickled through a row of tall buildings overlooking a checkered neon sign.

My parents adored it, inviting friends and family to gaze upon its splendor. And with good reason. The painting was exceptional.

They hung the painting in the living room, for all to see. There was no escaping it. Believe me, I tried. Something about it seemed wrong, like it could reach out and strangle you.

When it spoke to me, I nearly died.

"Hey, Joey," Tracy's painting said. "Get dead."

I approached with caution.

"Come live in my world, Joey," it chuckled. "Think you could handle it?" A shadow creature crawled out, exposing its teeth, then flew away.

I looked away faster than you can poop your pants. At twelve, I was too old to believe in the boogeyman, but young enough to be scared-to-death.

Over time, Tracy's paintings joined forces, conspiring against me. Sounds crazy, I know. But it's true. Some nights I'd hear them yammering back and forth, saying how ugly I was, and why nobody likes me. Their voices were unnaturally deep and always unpleasant. Why no one else heard them was beyond me. But I certainly wasn't gonna take this lying down.

When no one was home, I impaled the painting multiple times with a steak knife. It shrieked, pleading for me to stop. I didn't. Something grabbed my neck: the shadow creature. Snarling, it leapt teeth-first, sending me crashing onto the coffee table, spilling blood. The sight of blood made me berserk. With gritted teeth, I stabbed the wretched painting again and again, tearing it to shreds, until there was nothing left but blood, splattered like modern art.

Although my wounds were not life-threatening, the bloodstains were unforgiving. Scrubbing away, before my parents could catch me, Tracy's painting spoke.

"Hey, Joey," it scathed.

I turned and frowned.

There it was, hanging above the couch, growling. Below the checkered neon sign, a shadowy figure was leaning against a post, smoking.

"Hey, Joey," Tracy's painting said. "Get Dead."

The painting winked, blew a kiss, then vanished.

As time went on, Tracy's paintings started controlling her. Her behaviour was erratic. She had no friends, only painting. Whenever someone spoke to her, she lashed out. My parents thought it was a phase. "She's thirteen," they said. "She'll grow out of it."

They were dead wrong.

Tracy painted, each more elegant and sinister than its predecessor, until finally, she outdid herself. She'd painted a masterpiece. It was a collage of calico colours, blending a smoggy city skyline, with the Northern Lights. It was brilliant in its simplicity.

I hated it. Something about it was wrong. The painting seemed to have eyes, for starters. Plus, it was too good. As usual, everyone thought I was jealous. Little did they know.

I waited until she was asleep.

Her room was coffin-dark, smelling of stale meat. Tracy was asleep. Above her bed, the painting was making strange garbling sounds. Then it started spinning. I gulped. Before I could turn away, all three painting spoke at once:

"Hey, Joey," they said. "Get dead."

Livid, I flicked the light switch, illuminating the bedroom. Tracy's paintings fell with a thud, bouncing off her bed onto the floor.

Tracy snapped. "Buzz off, creep!"

"Buzz off, creep," the paintings repeated.

Three creatures crowded me at once, buzzing like banshees. Their hideous breath, sliding down my spine, making me gag. I bolted, never to set foot inside Tracy's bedroom again.

Graduation came at last, and soon I left for college. Life improved. I started socializing, making new friends. Then, during the holidays, my sister greeted me with a painting; it snapped like a crocodile, threatening to tear my left arm off. I hated it, I truly did. Problem was, I couldn't keep my eyes off it:..

Pitching on a mound of green, hand in weathered glove, hair blowing in the breeze, is twelve-year-old me; the crowd ballistic, waving signs and foamy fingers; the sweet smell of crackerjacks and freshly-grilled franks wafting through the summer air.

I locked Tracy's painting in the trunk of the car. Just to be safe. The following morning when I awoke, the damned painting was hanging in the living room, like it owned the place.

I stared, transfixed, not knowing what to make of it. The painting was remarkable, captivating. Should I leave it there? As I pondered, out came a shadow creature, barring its toothsome grin.

"Hey, Joey," it said. "Get dead."

I bolted. Soon thereafter, I moved to the other side of town, leaving Tracy's painting on the wall, where it could rot in Hell, for all I cared.

This story should end here. But it doesn't. It gets worse. And believe me, this is the Cole's Notes. I've left most of it out. Like the time my father was using the circular saw. Tracy's latest painting – an anonymous canoe wafting down a lazy river – was looming over him, seething.

The table saw fired up on its own, severing his thumb and index finger. Blood spilled everywhere. He was rushed to the hospital. Doctors were able to reattach them, but still…

That was long ago. These days, Tracy's paintings are being sold all over the world. In fact, you probably have one hanging in your home, or at the office. Hell, every dental office in America has one. Her work is quite extensive.

Tracy is a pseudonym. If she finds out I wrote this story, she'll send over another painting. Ugh. But that's not what concerns me.

It's you, Reader. You probably haven't put two and two together: that since coming into contact with Tracy's paintings, you're cursed. Even if you don't hear it talking, it does. Burn it, pray it doesn't return. Tracy's paintings are possessed. Each and every one of them. They hate people.

No wonder everyone is so agitated these days!

Beware The Bugs

Bugs.

Love em, hate em. Better get used to them. Because soon we'll be eating bugs for breakfast, lunch and dinner; deep fried, baked, barbecued, covered in chocolate or fresh off the grill. And not just those plump, juicy bugs either. Nope. I'm talking cockroaches, maggots, slugs, worms and snails, although I suppose some of you already eat snails, plus bugs that don't even exist yet.

How do I know this? Simple. I've been shown the future. But I'm just a teenager, right? What do I know? I'll tell you what I know, and you'd be wise to take heed. A great change is upon us. Except, there's nothing great about it. Horrific is more like it. Damnation, perhaps. In fact, our fate is so gruesome, I feel obligated to warn others, just as I've been warned. Take it or leave it, it's up to you.

The warnings arrived shortly after Dad left. I was seven. Lucky me. Over the years, Mom rarely spoke of Dad, and the few times I saw him, he seemed worried, like the weight of the world was resting upon his shoulders. Looking back, I can see why. Turns out, he knew things. Terrible things.

BEWARE THE BUGS

This was typed neatly on a note, and left in my lunch bag, jammed between two bologna sandwiches. I was in Grade Two. As you can imagine, I freaked out.

"Bugs?" my mind went berserk. "What bugs? I don't see any bugs!"

I scavenged through my lunch, searching for bugs, destroying the food in the process. Needless to say, I didn't eat that day. Instead, I went home hangry (hungry and angry), demanding answers from my unsuspecting mother, who threatened to call the school. Clearly, she had nothing to do with the note. Heck, we didn't even own a printer.

The next time it happened I was playing in the sandbox with Lyla, who lived in the unit next to us. Lyla ran home for some snacks. I followed her, giving her specific instructions on what cookies I preferred. She pushed me away, saying I was being annoying. Ouch. When I returned to the sandbox, something was scribbled in the sand:

BEWARE THE BUGS

My blood ran cold, my fists clenched into tiny balls of fury. Someone was lurking in the sandbox. But who? I looked everywhere, sure it was Buster, the local bully. But Buster was nowhere to be found. Neither was anyone else.

BEWARE THE BUGS

What did it mean? While searching the sandbox for bugs, Lyla returned, and handed me a Freezie. Then she jumped inside the sandbox, ruining the message. I was frazzled, and almost confided in her. It was on the tip of my tongue. But I never did. Even as a kid, I knew this topic was taboo.

By the time I reached middle school, the frequency of the warnings increased. Something I wasn't prepared for. Deep down, I figured they'd stop once I got older, thinking they were a figment of my overzealous imagination. If only this were true. One morning, for instance, I awoke to find a crisp, folded piece of paper placed neatly on my dresser. My heart fell to the floor. Someone had been lurking in my bedroom in the wee hours of the night. Someone or something. Cautiously, I crept along the creaky floor, toward the note. Then, I gasped.

BEWARE THE BUGS

Unlike the previous warnings, this one provided a photograph: filthy bugs with alien antennas and little legs for crawling; their beady black eyes peering at me, daring me to scream. I'd never seen such sickly creatures. I scurried to the washroom and vomited.

From then on, my life was riddled with anxiety. I even told my mother, who laughed and called me names. When I persisted, she threatened to take me to the doctor, whom I feared more than the bugs. Scared but undeterred, I stuffed the paper into a binder, and shoved it deep inside my closet. Not long later, it happened again. I came home from school, fatally exhausted and needing a nap, when I discovered the note hidden underneath my pillow:

BEWARE THE BUGS

Again, a picture was provided. These bugs seemed otherworldly, with their speckled eyes, sharp-looking shells, and crooked wings; they had long antennas that twisted tightly at the tips, like springs on a Pogo stick. Whatever they were, I didn't trust them. Not even close. What troubled me most was their claws, which could tear your eyeballs from their sockets. Questions crowded my inquisitive mind. Like, who put them there? And why? I was terrified. I longed for my mother to call the police. But she was too busy doing whatever it is adults do. So, I put the paper into the binder, and returned it to the closet. Then I tried to nap, which didn't go well. When sleep finally came, I was bombarded with nightmares; bugs as big as baseballs scurrying across my soft skin, scampering inside my nostrils, worming into my brain. I woke up screaming.

Sometime around Christmas, I got a surprise visit from my father, who came bearing gifts. I was thrilled. Underneath a stack of video games was a smattering of books. Being thirteen, I tossed the books aside, and went straight for the video games. Dad, who looked older than his years, treated us to tacos, and stayed the night. When I woke up, he was gone. That was the last time I saw my father. It wasn't until recently that I discovered the significance of those books.

High school was hell on earth. The other kids didn't like me. They still don't. To be fair, my high school career got off to a rough start. During week one, I was surprised by another warning: a locker full of bugs. Most were dead, but some of them were still alive, making crunching noises, which gave me the creeps. So much so, I puked all over myself. Oh, how the kids teased me, calling me terrible names. That's when I finally told Lyla. Big mistake. For her, this was the final straw. Our friendship was over. I won't go into detail, but by then she was hanging out with the Cool Crowd, leaving me alone to fend for myself.

The boggish warnings persisted; sometimes as random texts, or secretly-placed notes where only I'd discover them. Once, I stepped out of the shower, and BEWARE THE BUGS was scribbled on the steamy glass mirror. I shrieked. For starters, Mom wasn't home. I was alone. Not only that, the bathroom door was locked.

"Hello?" I called out, stupidly, not expecting an answer, but unable to stop myself. I quickly got dressed, then tip-toed across the apartment, looking for the culprit. The apartment was empty, and I soon gave up my search. Although I was growing increasingly anxious, never once did I question my own sanity. These warnings were real. Real as rain. Instead, I found solace in online gaming. Anything to keep my mind off bugs. This worked for a while. Kinda. Then something happened that changed everything. That day was December 31, 2022.

My mother threw a New Year's Eve party, inviting all of her friends. The party was a rager, but I was bored. Watching adults getting drunk and belligerent is not my idea of a good time, so I retreated to the confines of my bedroom, where another warning was lurking.

On my bed was the black book my father had given me some years earlier. It was open; the page showed a swarm of disgusting bugs, each varying in size and shape. Apparently, it was an encyclopaedia, dedicated solely to bugs. As I flipped through the glossy pages, completely grossed out, something came over me: a knowing. This book wasn't from our time. It was from the future. To be sure, I checked the publishing date. Just as I suspected: 2056.

I must've blacked out, because I awoke sometime later, just in time for the countdown. Mother and her friends were pretty lit by then, and they forced me out of bed. Afterwards, when I returned to my bedroom, two more books awaited me. One was paper thin; the other was a paperback. My hands trembled as I flipped through the skinny book, my eyes jumping from their sockets. This wasn't a book. It was a menu. A menu for eating bugs. It read:

Bed Bug Salad: $33.99. Chocolate-covered Cockroaches: 36.99. Centipede Cargo: $67.99. Beer Battered Blood Suckers: $69.99, A DEAL!!!

I gagged. This couldn't be true. But there it was. I felt hot and cold at the same time, my stomach in stitches. At the back of the menu was a brief description of the so-called restaurant: Grim Hoppers. I had to put it down. My mind couldn't handle it. Nor could my stomach. Besides, the other book was taunting me, with its orange cover, declaring two-o'clock. The book was The Time Traveler's Almanac.

Time travel? What does time traveling have to do with anything?

I riffled through the book at once, not tired in the slightest. To my surprise, my father's signature was on the inside, along with a note:

Best of luck, Zack!

Hope these books don't BUG you ☺

Love eternal, Dad

I nearly fainted. Everything suddenly made sense: My father was a time traveler. No wonder he was so mysterious. And old. He was trying to warn me. I wish he pulled me aside and told me. But then again, how does one confess such monstrosities?

I sent my father a series of emails, asking for more information. My emails remained unanswered, until recently, when he replied with a pair of articles, published July 9, 2042:

A GUIDE TO EATING BUGS; followed by: ARE BUGS THE NEW GOURMET?

The article scared me stupid. I'm still scared. Upon much consideration, I've decided not to disclose too much information. You see, I'm stuck between wanting to warn the public…more like shake them to the core…and not wanting to alter history. It's a paradox. One I could do without, thank-you-very-much.

But I will say this: I fear for our world. Why? Because we're on the brink of starvation. In the not-so-distant future, healthy food will be as sparse as gold coins. Something bad is on the horizon. Farmlands across the world will perish. Drought, famine, you name it. It's coming. Soon we'll be forced to eat…you guessed it… BUGS.

That's not the worse part. There's more. Just yesterday, my father sent another stark warning: A news article from 2083. Apparently, a bug-based diet has unexpected consequences: Human beings are mutating, turning into bugs, growing tentacles and other abnormalities. Our IQs have plummeted. We've become idiots.

Sorry, I wish this weren't true. But it is. That's why I'm giving you this warning. If only I was older, with more resources, maybe I could put a stop to this. But I'm only seventeen. Shit, I've still got another year of high school. So, with a heavy heart, I'll leave you with one final warning, same one I've been given time and time again:

BEWARE THE BUGS

Mrs. Whittaker's Mattress

I was completing my post grad. It didn't go well.

I moved into a fully furnished basement apartment, three blocks from school. The rent was unbelievable. I thought I'd hit the lottery. The old lady who lived upstairs was Mrs. Whittaker. She was sweet like lemon meringue pie. We hit it off straight away.

Then I started noticing red blotches on my legs. Oh how they itched. Scratching them made it worse, but it was impossible not to. I thought it was bed bugs, so I removed the sheets and checked the mattress. The mattress was a liquid chili massacre: brown blotches and swirling green splashes mixed with ketchup stains; the stains amalgamated into what looked like the shape of a body. When I flipped the mattress onto its side, I gagged. It looked like the after-effects of a deadly car crash.

I stared in disbelief, unable to comprehend how anyone would let a mattress get so bad. Finally, I scanned the mattress for bed bugs, and found none. Phew. One less thing to worry about. That weekend was spent preparing my speech to Mrs. Whittaker. How do I broach the subject of her deplorable mattress?

Mrs. Whittaker laughed nonchalantly when I brought it up. "Oh, that bed is fine and dandy," she assured me. "Always has been. Always will be."

I had my doubts. The old lady was an ocean of secrets. Most old people surround themselves with memories. Not Mrs. Whittaker. Her home was devoid of photographs. Plenty of jewellery, random knick-knacks and an old-fashioned TV with an antenna. But no family history whatsoever.

I didn't push the subject. We sat in her delectable kitchen, chatting. She wore a long apron and fuzzy orange oven mitts, and served up a batch of freshly-baked chocolate chip cookies with my name on them. All night, I stuffed my face with chocolate goodness. The cookies were delicious. We talked about nothing in particular, then I retreated to the basement to finish my latest assignment. It was 3am before my butt hit the bed. By then, I'd forgotten about the soiled mattress.

I awoke like a flash of lightning.

My legs felt prickly. No wonder. Something was crawling across them. Something big. Kicking and screaming, I thrashed about in a fit of rage, trying to get whatever it was off me. Then I fumbled for the bedside light. The basement gets spooky-dark at night. It took a minute for my eyes to adjust.

Frantically, I checked my mattress, finding no signs of bugs or creepy crawlers of any kind. Nothing. I forced myself to the washroom and peed for an eternity. Then I tip-toed across the living room, until I finally reached my bed. I searched the bed sheets like a detective, including the pillow cases. Checked under the bed. Twice.

Nothing.

Then a noise coming from the bathroom startled me.

"Um, hello?" I asked, not recognizing my own voice.

Silence. The only sound was my beating heart. Leaving the light on, I crawled under the covers, and scratched the red blotches until they bled. Sleep came slowly, like an old coffee maker that refuses to release its precious juice.

The following week, I was a disaster. Chuck, my best friend, was quick to point this out.

"You look like garbage," he told me, in between sips from a Styrofoam cup.

I laughed, then told him to take a leap off a tall building. He probed, but I wasn't ready to divulge my sullied little secret. It's just a dirty mattress, I reminded myself. If I hadn't removed the cover, I'd be none the wiser.

Except of course, I saw what lies beneath.

The spots on my legs worsened. Sleep was impossible. I'm a Light Sleeper (a curse, as any Light Sleeper can attest to). All I could do was lie awake and scratch, scratch, scratch. I looked and felt miserable. My concentration was non-existent. My test scores proved this. My mother was going to kill me if I flunked out of school. My final assignment, worth seventy percent of my final mark, was due in three weeks.

Things got worse.

One night, I heard something slithering across the floor: *SSSSLLLLLLLLZZZZZFFF.*

I snapped awake. On the floor, a dark shape was slithering into the washroom, slow and wet and gross.

"Just my imagination," I said, rubbing my weary eyes.

The toilet water splashed.

I tumbled out of bed, cracking my head on the night table. Then I followed a trail of sickly-green slime with red dots trickling leading toward the toilet.

"Hello?" I asked, knowing full well this question was in vain.

In reality, I was giving whatever-it-was time to escape. Out of site, out of mind, as they say. After an undisclosed amount of time, I forced myself off the floor and puttered to the washroom.

I shrieked.

Blood and puss were leaking from the toilet seat, dripping dime-sized drops onto the cold linoleum floor. Easily a pint's worth. The throne was as red as the devil's right hand. It was horrific.

I gathered some towels and soaked up the mess, elbow-deep in gruesome grime. The toilet seat kept sliding from side to side, refusing to cooperate. This was hard work. Sweat dripped into the rouge-tinted water like a leaky faucet: plunk, plunk, plunk.

Finally, three towels and two rolls of TP later, the gory mess was gone. By then it was 6am. Rise and shine! Sleepilly, I brewed some strong coffee and went to my desk, ready to work on my assignment.

Work never came.

Instead, I searched up bed bugs, night critters, midnight monsters, plus a plethora of demons, ogres, and evil-looking enemies. Each search provided terrifying results. By the time I finished, it was well past noon. I'd skipped my classes.

My school life was in shambles. My skin raging red. I needed to get to the bottom of this, and fast, before I flunked out of school.

"I should check the mattress again," I told myself tepidly. "Just in case."

I tore off the covers, and gasped. There's not enough alcohol in this world to make me forget the horror.

The mattress was a road map leading to Hell. The corpse-sized encrustation had turned a deeper hue. The crepuscular cracks running along its sides cut deep and wide. But that's not all. What made me want to crawl into a hole and never come out was the splotches of dried blood sullying the entire mattress. In the centre of the blood-soaked humanoid stain was a large black splotch. It looked like a tarantula, and was pulsing like a beating heart. Exactly where I slept.

The mattress, it seemed, was alive.

I stood transfixed, staring at the beating heart, unsure of what to make of it. Then I panicked. I considered calling my mother, in hopes of her valuable advice, but I stopped myself. My mother was going through a sticky divorce. Did I really want to worry her? My father lived a million miles away, and was preoccupied with his work. He'd tell me to figure it out myself. Honestly, I wouldn't blame him. I wasn't a kid anymore.

The scabs on my legs were infected. Pink patches of pestilence skittered up my legs like rattlesnakes. Anymore scratching, I'd rip the skin right off. Making matters worse, my studies were in jeopardy. And I was broke. Buying a new bed was out of the question. Even if I did, I couldn't toss out Mrs. Whittaker's old mattress. What would I tell her?

Last year I roomed with Chuck. But that was no longer an option. He was shacked up with his girlfriend Tessa, who hates me. Tessa hates everyone, but still. I was running out of options. I searched up other rooms for rent, but came up empty-handed. All the good places were taken. The rest were out of my price range.

One night, while tossing and turning in the middle of the night, the mattress started leaking. Something deplorable was being ejected. It clasped onto my legs, forcing me inside the mattress. It growled like a grizzly. Fighting for my life, I kicked and thrashed until it released me. Then I grabbed my knife. It was as dull as my depleted sense of humour, but it would have to do.

I crept closer to the mattress, which was bobbing up and down, bubbling like a pot of stew, releasing an odour resembling a corpse stuffed with strong cheese. Its heart was beating: *tha-dump, tha-dump, tha-dump.* White-knuckling the knife, I lunged, stabbing the mattress repeatedly. The mattress jerked and garbled, then went still. I stared at the disfigured stain on the mattress for an uncomfortable amount of time. The knife never left a mark.

Knife pointing, I waited. Finally, after the mattress monster failed to return, I freshened up as best I could, then walked to school. I felt horrible. My plan was to see the nurse about my rash, which was spreading across the rest of my body. The itch was insatiable.

"Well, well." A familiar voice called out. "Look who decided to show up for a change."

It was Chuck. Beside him was his girlfriend. Tessa rolled her eyes and quickly looked away. "Let's go, Chuck," she snapped.

Chuck patted my shoulder, before disappearing into the crowded hall. Tepidly, I stood outside the school's medical centre, not entering. Ultimately, I chickened out. The last thing I wanted was someone poking and prodding my flaky skin. They'd start asking questions. Questions I wasn't prepared to answer. Not yet, anyways. Instead, I returned home, where I was greeted by Mrs. Whittaker.

"Oh, there you are, Cameron," she said, carrying a tray of steaming biscuits.

My tummy grumbled. Instead of bringing up the elephant in the room – or dare I say the monster in the mattress? – I stuffed my face with fresh biscuits, washing them down with a tall glass of cold milk. I ate voraciously. Whenever I tried to broach the stingy subject, she would go off about the weather, or her baking, or how her backyard still needed mowing. Not once did she mention her past.

We spent the evening watching old reruns on her outdated television, and by nine o'clock, Mrs. Whittaker was fast asleep on her favourite reclining chair. Against my better judgement, I sneaked into her bedroom, quiet as a corpse in a coffin.

Her room stank of old-lady perfume and mould. Beside her bed, next to the oldest sewing machine I'd ever seen, was a large wooden box. Feeling like the World's-Worst-Person, but not caring, I inched closer. Mrs. Whittaker mumbled something.

I froze.

She was looking at me, but her eyes remained shut. The floorboard creaked as I crept ever closer. Then with two large strides, I reached the box. It was cracked oak, with gold markings carved into its hinges. A faded red strip ran along its side. With shaky hands, I opened the box. I gasped. Then I slammed the lid shut and beelined it for the basement, huffing and puffing and freaking out.

The box was stuffed the bones of the dead.

My mind went into lockdown. I uncorked a bottle of wine my mother had given me. The sound set off a series of silent alarms throughout my body. At first, I didn't know what to do. I don't typically drink red wine, but exceptions can be made. I drank the entire bottle in under an hour, chatting to myself like a drunken, deranged lunatic.

"I should scoot upstairs and put the old lady's room back in order," I whispered to myself, in between gulps of red. I pondered this for an inconceivable length of time, while stealing sips from the bottle. Ultimately, I stayed where I was. Fear had stolen over me. I wasn't going anywhere.

Having a low tolerance for alcohol, I was absolutely inebriated. At some point, after finishing the bottle, I crawled my way under the bed sheets and crashed for the night. I awoke in the morning with an ear-splitting headache. My legs were burning. My hands and arms covered in itchy red spots. When I touched my inflamed skin, blood oozed out. The pain was insidious.

I flew out of bed, scurrying to the bathroom. The reflection in the mirror wasn't encouraging. I applied heavy amounts of cream on my sores, feeling little relief. When I returned, there was a trail of mucus slinking towards my bed like a slaughtered snail.

That was the final straw.

I texted my mother, telling her I was dropping out of school, that I could finish my post grad in the fall. I was still young. Time, as they say, was on my side.

My mother called back immediately, wanting none of this. But once she heard the distress in my voice, she sent money for a bus ticket home. I packed up my belongings like my life depended on it. Because it did. It didn't take long, seeing as I owned next to nothing but a laptop, some clothes, and an array of overpriced textbooks as big as my current crisis.

The bus schedule was not promising. That said, I had no intention of waiting here. Upstairs, Mrs. Whittaker was swearing like a trucker on amphetamines, making a commotion. Her feet were elephants thumping the floor.

She knew.

Scared and delirious, I raced upstairs, dashing towards the door.

Mrs. Whittaker was blocking the exit. Her wrinkled neck pulsating purple veins. Standing a mere five-foot-nothing, with white dishevelled hair and meatless frame, she was an incredible site to behold.

"Cameron," she said, in a quivering voice. "You've been a bad, bad boy."

She was pointing a gun. The gun was as old as the stains on my mattress.

My eyes looked past her, at the door.

Mrs. Whittaker snarled. "You ain't going nowhere, sonny boy." She cocked the gun. "I've got plans for you."

She motioned me into the kitchen. The clicking of the colt made me pick up the pace. Maybe her ancient-looking pistol was as limp as wet noodle, but I wasn't feeling lucky enough to find out.

She told me to sit, so I did.

Immediately, my skin began to crawl. Every inch of my body was red-hot. I was in rough shape. What I wouldn't do for a scratch; to scrape my fingernails across my arms and legs, making the itch go away.

"Stay put," Mrs. Whittaker ordered.

The sweet smell of cranberry muffins wafted from the oven. My stomach turned. I terrible thought came at once: Maybe she was adding something to her pastries. Something sinister. Drugging me. At this point, all bets were off.

Mrs. Whittaker returned with rope. Then with remarkable speed, she bound my hands and legs. Before I could react, she'd duct taped my mouth shut. Clearly, she'd done this before.

Right before my eyes, Mrs. Whittaker transformed into something non-human. Her face was a leathery mask with empty spaces where her eyes, ears and mouth should be. She produced a large butcher's knife; it was a knife that could carve up a pumpkin.

"You've been infected," she said, while sharpening the knife: *SWOOSH; SHOOSH; SHOOSH; SWOOSH...*

Fear enveloped me. Who the hell was Mrs. Whittaker? And what's she planning on doing to me? My skin was like sandpaper. Desperately, I tried scratching my legs with my toes, resulting in me falling off the chair.

Mrs. Whittaker barely noticed. She kept sharpening the knife, regarding the silvery blade like it was a long-time friend. Judging by its well-worn wooden handle, it was.

Somehow, I returned to the chair, shifting in my seat until I was facing her bedroom. The box on the floor was open. A trail of brittle bones scattered like discarded toys.

"You've discovered my bone collection," she said with a simper. "Soon, you'll be added to my collection." Her pistol lay on the counter next to her, daring me to say otherwise.

Mrs. Whittaker advanced, sticking the knife against my throat. The prickly edge glistened under the fluorescent lights.

"Now," she croaked. "You die."

I gulped.

Knock; knock; knock.

Mrs. Whittaker stopped dead in her tracks.

Someone was at the door.

"Now, who could that be?"

She peaked around the corner, her face twisting in rage.

"Don't move."

She traded her knife for the gun.

Then she disappeared.

The door creaked as it opened. I heard a muffled voice, which I recognized.

Chuck barged into the kitchen, staring at me in bemusement, eyes jumping from me to the knife, back to me.

"Freeze!"

Mrs. Whittaker stuck the gun in his back.

Chuck spun around and drop-kicked the hag square in the head. Mrs. Whittaker crumbled like crumbs.

Chuck chortled. "Thirteen years of karate just so I could save my bro from the Wicked Witch of the West."

I burst into tears.

Chuck freed me. Things went blurry. I don't recall what happened next. All I know is that I was rushed to the hospital, where I remained for many months.

Word travelled fast. Turns out, Mrs. Whittaker was wanted for murder all across the country, and had been for many years. Her capture was front page news. Her notoriety spread fast.

Nothing was mentioned of Mrs. Whittaker's mattress.

Perhaps the mattress was her secret hiding spot. The source of her power. Dark magic, maybe.

Or something else altogether. I don't know. Chuck, to this day, still teases me about it.

Being the clever asshole he is, Chuck managed to snap some disturbing pics of Mrs. Whittaker's mattress, moments before the police and paramedics arrived.

On random nights, as my head hits the pillow, he'll send disturbing pics or GIFs or memes of the mattress. Then he'll with me goodnight. To Chuck, this is funny.

I forgive Chuck's taunting, seeing as how he saved my life. Turns out, my worried-sick mother messaged him after hanging up with me. Good thing. Otherwise, its of to Mrs. Whittaker's bone collection. Or worse: stuffed inside Mrs. Whittaker's mattress.

Funny thing happened: The morning after Mrs. Whittaker's capture, she vanished. Her holding cell was empty. She vanished without a trace. The security cameras prove this. In the wee hours of night, Mrs. Whittaker, fast asleep, sank deep into her mattress. At precisely six am, she vanished.

One thing is certain: This isn't the end of Mrs. Whittaker. Maybe she's living in someone's mattress. That's my guess. Maybe your mattress. Gross huh? You'd better check, just in case. Your mattress might be birthing something evil.

Mrs. Whittaker, perhaps.

Junk Drawer

My Secret started at my first apartment. That's when my stuff started disappearing. Small stuff, like guitar pics and cigarette lighters. (Yes, I was a smoker back then.)

"Where's my lighter?" I'd ask Dave, my roommate and best friend, whenever it went missing. Dave, who had a personalised gold Zippo lighter with his name engraved in fancy letters, had no time for such cheap, novelty items. Besides, Dave was a slob. He rarely, if ever, put his own stuff away. And he didn't play guitar. So, it wasn't him.

I shrugged it off. Who cares, right? Except, my stuff kept disappearing. Sure enough, every time I lost something: a lighter, toothbrush, my wallet – you get the picture – it would always end up in the drawer closest to the fridge: The Junk Drawer.

My girlfriend Brenda, a total neat-freak, who unofficially moved in with me, became my number-one suspect.

"Why do you keep putting my stuff in the drawer?" I'd ask, one-hundred percent convinced of her guilt.

Her denial was adamant. She'd bat her pretty eyes and tell me to go stuff myself. Needless to say, I assumed it was her, but again I shrugged it off. Maybe this was Her Thing. Her peculiarity. We've all got one, right? Back then, I was only mildly concerned. I mean, at least I knew where to look. It became a running joke.

The joke was on me.

Let's fast forward a few years, shall we? Brenda was long gone, thinking I was a wacko, and. Dave grew weary of My Secret, as he called it, worrying his stuff would inevitably go missing. Ultimately, he moved back home with his parents, and that was the end of our First Apartment.

I presumed My Secret had run its course. By then, I was earning decent money, and could afford a better apartment in a safer neighbourhood. My first Monday at the place, my alarm hadn't gone off. How could it? My trusted alarm clock, which I'd owned since a child, was nowhere to be seen.

There's nothing worse than waking up late for work on a Monday morning. Panicking, I trudged towards the kitchen, grumpy and confused. When I opened the drawer closest to the fridge: Voila! my alarm clock.

"Not again," I groaned, as a dreadful feeling sank to the pit of my stomach. "This can't be happening."

Maybe I was a sleepwalker. Seemed plausible. Except, if I was, surely someone would've noticed by now. Brenda, no doubt. No, it wasn't that. So, who (or what) was stealing my stuff? I lived alone. There was no one here but me.

There was no rhyme or reason as to how often my stuff would go missing, but one thing kept consistent: my stuff only disappeared while I was asleep. This made me uneasy. It brought about too many questions. Disturbing questions with scary answers, no doubt.

Cue the insomnia.

By my mid-thirties, My Secret started growing teeth. By then, I was renting the main floor of a house. Taylor, my latest girlfriend, was at her wit's end. She thought I was possessed by the devil.

It was a pillow, of all things, that finally made her leave me. She'd spent the night, as she did most weekends, and when we woke up, her pillow was gone. I checked around the bed. Nothing. Then I marched into the kitchen. Her pillow was stuffed into the Junk Drawer like a jack-in-the-box, all cranked up and ready to erupt, which it did, as soon as I opened the drawer.

Via text, Taylor dumped me, saying she no longer felt safe around me. Honestly, I couldn't blame her. I didn't feel safe around me either. Especially at night, when my stuff goes missing.

Life went on as it does, and a year or so later I met Ashley. We hit it off right away. I thought she was The One. Our first night together, I was a nervous wreck. Talk about pressure. Please don't let anything go missing, I prayed. Oh, please.

Something did.

Her bra went missing. It should've been lying on the floor, next to the bed, where she'd left it. But it wasn't. Her bra was gone. She thought I was playing a childish prank, having a laugh at her expense. If only that was the case. My stomach sank. I really liked Ashley. This could ruin everything.

With feet like hammers, I charged into the kitchen and opened the Junk Drawer. There it was: Ashley's bra. This was the first time something that wasn't mine ended up here. Not good. How do I return the bra while convincing her I'm not the World's Biggest Creep?

In the end, Ashley forced the truth out of me. And to my surprise, she believed me. Her grandmother, she said, was haunted by ghosts most of her life. Ashley wouldn't go into detail, but I could tell she was intrigued, and resolute to get to the bottom of this. And that's exactly what she did, for better or for worse. Under her guidance, we started monitoring these idiosyncrasies.

We set up surveillance.

Then we waited.

At first, nothing happened; or more accurately, nothing disappeared. I nearly died of embarrassment. It wasn't until the following weekend that my newly-acquired iPad went missing. When I awoke, it wasn't on my bedside table where it should've been. Take a guess where it was.

When I checked the video, the video proved nil. Nothing touched the drawer. When I opened it, My iPad simply appeared, like it had been there all alone. None of this made any sense.

"What if we keep the drawer open at night?" she asked.

A good idea.

The following weekend, I woke up missing my pants. I'd left them on the back of the computer chair before going to bed. Now, they're gone.

The Junk Drawer.

Wearing only boxers, I raced to the kitchen, but Ashley beat me to it. She was trembling, clearly perturbed, pale as paper. Something was wrong.

"Watch this," she said, barely above a whisper. "You're not going to believe it."

Ashley pressed play.

For a few minutes nothing happened; at 6:06 a.m. my pants suddenly appeared, stuffed neatly in the drawer.

"No way."

We watched the video over and over and over; 6:05: No pants. 6:06: Pants. Every time. Ashley zoomed in, analysing it in every possible way, but there was no logical explanation.

Out of desperation, Ashley's BFF gave us a Ouija board. Ashley was bewitched, excited to try something new. I, on the other hand, was sceptical.

"Thanks, but no thanks," I said. "This is my life we're dealing with. I've got enough problems."

Naturally, I was outvoted.

I could've fought harder, but I didn't. Keeping Secrets takes a toll. That's what they do. Of course, the severity of Keeping Secrets varies; some secrets are dangerous, potentially life-threatening. Mine was manageable, or so I thought.

Enter: Ouija board.

"D-d-do you have a name?" I stuttered stupidly.

It was the first thing that popped in my head; I mean, somebody had to say something. It was me and Ashley and her BFF, our bodies bunched together under candlelight. We were giggling, nervous and anxious about getting started. When our hands met, all the doors slammed simultaneously.

We gulped. Something was in the kitchen. Something evil. We all felt it. Hands trembling, we guided the planchette toward the letter J; the letter A, followed by C; subsequently, forming JACOB. The room gasped.

"I don't know anyone named Jacob," I blurted out.

"Ask it another question," Ashley whispered shakily, nudging me with her elbow.

I did, and once I started, I couldn't stop:

"Who's Jacob? And why is he stealing my stuff? And how do I make him stop stealing My Stuff?"

The lights turned off, the table started shaking, then the Ouija board burst into flames. Apparently, Question Time was over. Ashley's BFF went dashing for water, and put out the fire. I was sulking. The Ouija board lay in ruins, as did my love life.

The following day Ashley said she no longer feels safe around me. She called it off. It was déjà vu all over again. After the breakup, I was alone, yet again. But it's for the best, right?

Except that's not entirely true. I was not alone. I had Jacob to contend with. Jacob and the Junk Drawer. Just what I needed. Before long, items I'd lost as a teenager started showing up. My old baseball card, a Mark McGuire sophomore, a real treasure. Growing up, McGuire was my favourite baseball player. Seeing and holding the card again brought a wave of unexpected sentimentality. Teary-eyed, I removed the card from the plastic sleeve and studied it carefully. It was exactly like how I remembered it: the sharp look stamped across McGuire's face, the slight crease on the left corner, just above the Athletics' logo.

Impossible.

The following week it happened again, only this time it was my very first wallet; equipped with five bucks and a fresh-looking condom. I'd lost it twenty years ago. When it was brand new. As teenagers, me and Dave set out for burgers, and being recently employed and feeling we've earned it, we overindulged, ordering two of everything, spending the better part of two hours eating and belching and being belligerent. Leaving, I accidentally threw my wallet into the garbage, along with the rest of the biodegradable heap, never to be seen again.

Until now.

I opened it. That new leather smell hit me straight away. The damp, intoxicating aroma wafting through nostrils like a rolling fog of an autumn mist.

This can't be real.

"Jacob!" I stunned myself with my velocity. "Where did you find this?"

No answer.

"Tell me where it came from!" My voice rose to a fervour.

Silence.

Something inside me finally snapped. I became unhinged, no longer trusting anyone or anything. People noticed; namely my boss, who made me take a month's leave of absence. I shrugged. Maybe I could finally get to the bottom of this. The problem was: I didn't know where to begin. I was searching for ghosts.

A visit to my parent's was in order.

After a lengthy discussion with my mother, I was convinced she knew something. Upon mentioning My Secret, Mother's eyes lit up. Maybe it was my imagination. My mother has an exceptional poker face.

My father, on the other hand…

"Son," my father said in his gruff voice. "I think it's time we have ourselves a talk."

He fetched a bottle of Cognac, then led me to the den, where we talked for the better part of the evening. His words chilled me to the bone.

"Your great-grandfather was a war hero." His eyes were far away. "I'm talking World War One. He almost died. Shoulda died too, some say. Got shot up pretty bad. But something saved him. "Not a lot is known about your great-grandfather. My father, your grandfather, refused to talk about the man. What I do know is this: When Gramps came back from the Great War, he came back different: cruel and nasty. Always playing outlandish pranks on people. And his ingenuity knew no bounds."

I was stunned, knowing nothing of my great-grandfather. In fact, this was the first I'd ever heard of him. I was on the edge of my seat, as my father took me further down the rabbit hole. When he revealed my great-grandfather's name, I nearly died.

"Jacob Starr died at 58. Poor bastard didn't reach 60. From all accounts, the townsfolk threw a party on his behalf. You see, nobody liked Jacob Starr. Not one bit. Many years later, my grandmother made a deathbed confession about the man. I chose not to believe her. Truth is: I didn't want to believe her. But deep down I knew she was telling the truth."

My father abruptly stopped, and poured himself a drink, still lost in Memory Lane. His hair was silver and fine, his face ravaged with wrinkles, but his eyes were blazing. I, on the other hand, was terrified.

"Jacob Starr?" I gulped.

"Yes, of course," my father said, clearly startled. "I must've mentioned him to you before."

He hadn't, but judging from the weary look he was giving me, I wasn't about to bring this up. My father took another drink, then continued.

"After the war, Jacob Starr opened a magic shop, dealing mostly with black magic and the occult. That's where he met your grandmother. According to her, Jacob could move through time and space, a trick he acquired during the Battle of Passchendaele; he stepped on a landmine – though it may have been a grenade, or the wrong end of a gun, I can't remember – and while his body moved through the muddy air, he slipped into another dimension.

"He opened a portal – a door to the Other Side. My grandmother believed he's still there. Being a pest. She said her stuff began disappearing after he passed - reappearing in her attic."

I was shaking. This was not what I was expecting to hear.

"B-but, what does this have to do with my disappearing stuff? Why does my stuff always end up in the same drawer? And why is my old stuff starting to show up?"

Again, my father went quiet. He simply stared into his glass, ignoring the world around him. Just as I thought he would ignore my question, he spoke up. "Well now, those are some loaded questions, wouldn't you say?"

Indeed, they were.

"I'm sorry son. I don't have any suitable answers. I've been asking myself those same questions for years."

That caught my attention. Suddenly, my father's apprehensiveness made sense.

"This happened to you as well," I said. It was written all over his face.

My father nodded. "Started when I turned twenty," he told me. "I thought I was going bonkers. Maybe I was. Your mother seemed to think so. It kept happening. I was livid, let me tell you. Your mother nearly left me."

My father lowered his head, shamefully, then refilled his glass. "I hid this from you as best I could," he added. "I mean, it was mostly harmless. Just spooky as goddamn hell.

"One time, I lost my entire Beatles collection on 8-Track. That pissed me off. Your mother, of course, was glad to see them disappear. She hated rock and roll. But I got the last laugh. I knew where to find them."

"The Junk Drawer," I said.

"Precisely," he said. "Except in my case: my closet."

We spoke for hours. This was the longest time we'd spent together in years. We inevitably changed topics, but before I left, my father divulged one last piece of information: that since I'd moved away, his stuff stopped disappearing.

Alas, the torch had been passed to me.

I left feeling reinvigorated yet deeply disturbed. If my deceased great-grandfather was rummaging through my belongings, how was I to stop him? Or make a truce?

I considered finding an exorcist – if that's even a thing – but decided against it. I'd had enough with the dark forces. Besides, it's not like I was waking up with REDRUM painted over my walls in blood or anything. Jacob was a prankster. Did he really learn the secret of eternal life? And if so, why was he hiding my stuff? Certainly, he could come up with more interesting ways to spend his immortality.

I became increasingly aware of Jacob's presence. In fact, he became my unofficial roommate. I'd reach for the bar of soap in the shower – gone. Same goes for my shaving cream, my brush, my favourite coffee mug, small stuff, but still. It was super-annoying. Things finally hit a tipping point.

The final straw was when my car keys disappeared. I checked everywhere, including the Junk Drawer. Then I threw a tantrum. This was my first day back to work, and my car keys were missing. I tossed everything inside the junk drawer onto the floor, then stomped the stupid drawer into a million pieces. I should've done this sooner.

In desperation, I tried pleading with Jacob, begging him to be reasonable. It was my first day back to work after my leave of absence, I must arrive on time. Jacob remained silent. Think! I told myself. There *must* be a new hiding spot. I searched everywhere, tearing my house apart in the process. I didn't have time for this.

My keys were nowhere to be found.

I ordered an Uber, kicking myself for not owning a spare set of car keys, and arrived late to work. I was miserable. My cell phone vanished the following week. My fists were knotted balls of rage. I could've killed Jabob. Then paranoia settled in.

What next? I imagined the worst.

As if on cue, the following morning my car went missing. I would've called the police, but my phone was still MIA. Things were spiralling out of control. I didn't have enough resources to be constantly replacing my stuff. Phones are expensive. So are cars. Reluctantly, Dave called the cops.

The police arrived asking questions, none of which I had any answers to. Ultimately, I was dragged into the police station for further questioning. After a long ordeal, an officer produced surveillance footage of my driveway. This did nothing to increase my trust in law enforcement. That said, I watched in complete and utter shock as the officer showed me the footage.

"Watch this," the officer said without emotion.

I watched.

It was an otherwise inert morning. The birds were warming up their throats in song, the orange sun settling upon the budding boulevard. Nobody was near my driveway, not even a squirrel. Yet at precisely, 6:07 a.m. my car vanished into thin air. Gone, just like that.

I felt sick to my stomach. My mind was on the blink. I could tell the officer was equally perplexed. Neither of us had a valid explanation.

My father showed up later that night. To my amazement, he rode in my car, claiming it arrived unannounced, keys in the ignition. He tried calling me, but I wouldn't answer my phone. Ugh. I could've killed someone right then.

We examined my car thoroughly. My phone was in the glove compartment, dead. Not only that, my old hockey bag was in the truck, rotting like left-over garbage from a dumpster. You'd think a dead body was inside it. I certainly wasn't going to check.

Reluctantly, my father handed me the only remaining picture of Jacob Starr. I was stunned, seeing my great-grandfather sharply dressed in a WW1 military uniform, with a smug sneer stretched across his stern and chiselled face. His resemblance to me was striking.

After driving Dad home, I placed the black and white photograph of Jacob Starr in the living room as a peace offering. Maybe, just maybe this would work.

. . .

So far, so good. A month has passed and I haven't lost anything. At home, that is.

Problem is: I'm losing stuff at work: Pens, staplers, pencils, and such. They always end up in the bottom drawer of my desk. Last week it was a co-worker's laptop. I had a helluva time trying to explain that one. Then it was my data report on my Big Project, shortly after I'd submitted it.

So, there's that.

My coworkers are asking questions. Reluctantly, and with my back against the wall, I told them about Jacob Starr. What choice did I have? Janice, the woman whose laptop vanished, only to be discovered in the bowels of my office desk, was intrigued. After weeks of sleuthing, she discovered something unexpected. Something new to keep me up at night.

Turns out, the century-old building I work at once housed a magic shop named Starr Light Starr Bright. Rumours of Aleister Crowley frequenting the shop run rampant. My co-worker even managed to dig up the proprietor's name: Jacob Starr.

So, there's that.

The Grolf

Grandpa told us many stories. Most of him as a strapping young lad, fighting off Nazis and commies and saving our hides (his words, not mine). But then there were his 'other stories'. The ones he'd tell us late at night, after he'd 'had a few'. Typically, we'd be at the cottage, surrounded by lake and stars, when Grampa talked of The Grolf.

The Grolf, Grandpa told us, was a wolf-like monster lurking in the vast forests of Northern Ontario, the final destination for such creatures. It was long and lean, with teeth like swords and claws like Freddie Kruger. Tara, my older sister, was enthralled. I, on the other hand, was terrified.

Then Grandpa got sick. Lung cancer came swift as morning rain. "Cancer sticks finally got the best of me," he'd say, puffing away on his never-ending cigarette. Tara wouldn't stop crying. She was always Grandpa's favourite. They were like two peas in a pod.

As Grandpa lay dying, wrapped in his favourite duvet, family by his side, he told us one last story.

"The Grolf is REAL," he said, while hacking up a lung. "But it only comes out on very special occasions. You must remember this."

We leaned in, ignoring the stench of death permeating from his entire orifice.

"And it MUST be stopped. Once and for all."

Grandpa stopped for a sip of water, his withered hands barely able to hold the glass. Not surprisingly, he refused our help.

Tara, now sixteen, was clutching my hands, tears leaking from her forest-green eyes. I'd never seen her so sad.

"There," he pointed. "Look out the window." His voice was like a chainsaw. "Tell me what you see."

We peered out the cottage window. It was a gorgeous view. Fallen leaves blanketed the forest floor; golden rays of autumn sun trickled through tall trees. The morning moon hung over the lake like a silhouette. A stubborn rain cloud draped high above us, sprinkling us with delicate showers. Then a rainbow appeared, filling the sky with a banquet of delight. A Hallmark moment if there ever was one.

Grandpa snapped. "This is it! The time of the Grolf! When the sun and moon meet, it's raining, and there's a rainbow." A lifetime of memories loomed behind Grandpa's dying eyes. Then his face turned serious. "The Grolf only appears under these circumstances."

Tara's grip on my hand tightened; her eyes as wet as water. Deep down, we thought he was delirious, but this was our final moment with him, so we surrendered to it.

Our parents brought snack into the room. Mother was all worked up about something Dad did. I didn't care. I was thirteen. My parents' squabbling was the furthest thing from my mind.

Grandpa succumbed to sleep. It would be his last. He died peacefully that evening. Meanwhile, reports of a gruesome animal attack started pouring in. Apparently, some hikers set out along the Muskoka Trails, the day Grandpa died, and never returned. Their cell phones were discovered next to a pile of gristly bones.

As usual, it was deemed a bear attack.

Tara and I knew better.

"The Grolf," she gasped, wide-eyed. "It was true all along."

I didn't believe this, but was too sad and scared to say so. The following summer we returned to our northerly cottage. Tara, who'd recently graduated from high school, was set to attend veterinary school in the fall. Grandpa left plenty of money, which easily covered the costs. Despite my protests, Tara brought her boyfriend Carl, whom I disliked immensely. Carl was a turd. With his greasy black hair and ever-present earbuds jammed into his oversized ear canals. His nasally voice and shifty eyes couldn't be trusted. Oh, how I longed for it to be just the two of us again.

One morning, he and Tara set out on canoes, and crossed the lake. They were to spend the afternoon having a picnic, doing God-knows-what.

They never returned.

The weather was foreboding. The sun and moon fought like foes, the rain drizzling in droves; a rainbow kissed the ominous sky. I shuddered. Grandpa's warnings returned like a cycle of bad dreams.

"The Grolf."

My parents were going berserk. They phoned the police, who with the help of a team of locals, set out on a search-and-rescue mission, lasting long through the night.

Tara and Carl's belongings were discovered on a small slice of beach. Blood and gore soaked the sand. Not far away, was a pile of fleshy bones and matted fur.

My mother was heartbroken, beyond repair. The following night, she drowned herself in the lake, leaving me and my father alone to fend for ourselves.

It was the worst summer of my life. I'm still haunted by it. Some nights Tara visits me in my dreams, dead and decomposed, whispering warnings of the toothsome monster. Other nights it's Grandpa, his voice as sharp as razors. "You MUST kill the Grolf," he'll say, before dissolving into darkness. I awake in a pool of sweaty sheets, longing for the days of my youth. The days before the sorrow.

After high school, I got a job as a welder, and soon formed my own family. My wife Sarah and our lovely daughter Lyla were my pride and joy. They kept my days bright and my nights worry-free. Sadly, tragedy was lurking, waiting for the proper conditions to arise.

Last year, we vacationed at the old cottage. I'd spent the previous summer doing renovations and repairs, until it was shipshape. Lyla, who'd just turned twelve, was thrilled. She was the envy of her friends. Against my better judgement, she brought her two besties: Brie and Bryce, who were twins, and sweet as roses.

One morning, while Lyla and I were fishing off the dock, Brie and Bryce sneaked off to go exploring.

We never saw them again. "Where's the twins?" my wife asked, while barbecuing burgers.

I shrugged. They were here a minute ago. I looked at Lyla, who was beaming, having just caught three small-mouth bass. Thunder crackled in the distance. Rain sprinkled like fireflies. The morning moon yawned. Then the sun appeared from behind a grey cloud.

Fear stole over me. Soon a rainbow would appear. I grabbed my wife and daughter, and hurried them inside the cottage. At once, Lyla burst into tears, crying for her friends. My wife was giving me a look that could sink a fleet of ships.

"What's wrong, Richard?" she asked, using her don't-lie-to-me tone.

My mind crashed. My gaping mouth ajar. No answers came. Do I mention Grandpa's tall tales? The monster that only appears under specific circumstances; circumstances that have now arisen?

No fucking way.

Only a small part of me believed in the Grolf; the fraction of mind clinging to childhood. The rest of me declared: Monsters don't exist. Especially the Grolf. I checked the time: The twins had been missing for almost an hour.

Lightning lit the sky like fireworks.

My wife's glare changed to: You'd better do something. Quick.

I called up our closest neighbours, Dave and Rowan, asking for help. Dave, a mountain of a man, came over straight away. He's an ex-marine, and came heavily armed. I recoiled, being nervous of such weapons. Hell, I'd never even bagged a deer (a right of passage in the north). I was as green as grass.

"Do as I do." Dave ordered.

He showed me how to load, cock and carry a rifle. We prepared some food and drink, then set off through the winding forest. The grim realisation that the twins may be dead was growing stronger by the second. I considered mentioning the Grolf, but chickened out. Adults don't speak of monsters. And I wasn't about to change that. We hiked in silence, until a raging roar echoed off the lake, bringing us to a halt.

Dave's face grew dim.

"Be careful," he said, in a gruff voice. He produced a hunting knife that could carve a crocodile. He looked scared, which made me feel uneasy. This is a man who's seen combat.

"Tell me again, Rick," he said slowly, as if speaking to a child. "When did they disappear?"

"Two hours ago," I said in a shaky voice. "Tops."

Dave gazed at the sky and frowned. His face hardened as he spoke. "Probably," he said. "Your daughter's friends are dead."

Tears drizzled down my face like a leaky faucet. I wiped them as casually as a cat climbing a tree. Meanwhile, Dave continued studying me. We stood toe-to-toe for an uncomfortable length of time, before he finally spoke up. What he said nearly killed me.

"You KNOW, don't you?"

My face turned milk-white.

"Excuse me?"

Dave's fists bulged like boxing gloves.

"Don't play dumb with me, Rick. I know more about you than you think."

As I gazed into his fearsome eyes, marvelling in his massiveness, he said the two words I feared most:

"The Grolf."

I started choking; spittle and snot flew like firecrackers from my sullied face.

Dave snarled. "Get it together, Rick! This is serious!"

I pulled myself together, as best I could under these extraordinary circumstances, and told him of Grandpa's stories. Dave nodded approvingly. Turns out, our grandfathers were once pals, having served together in the war. I couldn't believe it. Then again, here I was, a middle-aged man, hunting a creature who only appears when the moon and sun are out, it's raining, and there's a rainbow.

We marched along the beaten path, calling for Brie and Bryce, until our voices grew hoarse.

"There's something your grandpa didn't tell you," Dave declared, while leading me through the thick of the trees. "The only way to kill the beast is by decapitating it."

I gulped.

Dave continued. "Then – and this is the important part – you must bury its head as far away as possible. Otherwise, the head and body will reattach, and it'll re-emerge, stronger than ever. Burning the beast won't work either. Believe me. I've tried."

We hiked. Sweat was beating down my face and my legs were growing tired. I drank sparingly from the canteen, trying to keep up, praying for this nightmare to end.

As we neared an anonymous stretch of beach, Dave stopped. "There!" he pointed.

A child's knapsack was scattered across the foliage. We hurried over. Brie's backpack was painted in blood. Her sneakers shredded beyond repair.

Thunder boomed in the distance. The wind intensified.

Dave trembled. "Time to go."

Feeling utterly dejected, I followed him back to the main trail. Dave's eyes never left the sky, which boasted a battlefield between sinister-looking clouds and tranquil-blue sky. As the clouds parted and the sun reappeared, a drop of rain splashed my forehead. When the moon peeked its head from behind a cloud, something stirred in the bushes.

Dave cocked his rifle.

I looked up and gasped. Stretching across the lake like the arm of an angel, was a rainbow. A series of gruesome growls skipped across the lake.

"The Grolf."

Dave dove behind a fallen tree, taking cover. I gawked. Without warning, something lunged at me, seemingly from nowhere, and I was knocked unconscious. Darkness engulfed me, as I dissolved into nothingness.

Shots rang out, as loud as rockets.

My eyes suddenly opened. I turned. The beast was charging towards Dave, baring its treacherous teeth. It was fully-erect, with gangly arms and thick, greasy fur; its deadpan eyes devoid of life. The thing was translucent, and moving at an incredible speed.

Dave open-fired.

Blood and gore spewed from the beast's brute body. But the thing didn't deter. Instead, it toppled Dave, stealing his weapon as one might take candy from a toddler.

Dave fought diligently, but to no avail.

I watched horrified as the Grolf mounted Dave, tearing him apart. That snapped me out of my fog. My fingers found the trigger. I took a knee, said a silent prayer, aimed and fired. BAM. The rifle's kickback knocked me flat on my ass.

The shot rang true. I hit the beast square in the head. The Grolf collapsed, blood and gristle leaking from its blown-apart brains. Dave, to my astonishment, jumped on top of it, and cut the creature's head clean off. Its body deflated like a beach ball, laying dormant on the crimson-coloured sand.

"We did it," Dave declared, wiping the blood from his bayonet. "Well done, Rick."

Dave looked haggard. Clearly, he needed an ambulance. I gazed upward. At that moment, the sky cleared, the rain ceased, the rainbow dissolved into emptiness. The moon disappeared, until the following night, where it hung like an omen, orange and speckled.

"We're not done yet," Dave said.

He led us back to the cottage, where he grabbed a large sack from his boat. He plopped the Grolf's head into it, and we set out to bury it.

I dug the deepest hole imaginable. It took over an hour. I was fatally exhausted. My hands and knees were incapacitated. A deep depression devoured me, while Dave dropped the bag into the hole.

"We'll toss the body into the middle of the lake," Dave said, looking worse for wear.

"Sounds like a plan."

Except when we returned, the headless corpse was gone.

Dave shook his head, his face twisting in anger.

"How could I be so stupid," he repeated, over and over.

We returned to the cottage without saying a word. My family greeted us with worried-sick faces.

I made up a story and they pretended to believe it. The police set up another search and rescue. The bones of Brie and Bryce were found nearby. This added to my daughter's demise. She's never been the same since. We left the following day and never returned. Dave was rushed to the hospital. We never spoke again.

Thus, the legend lives on.

Whatever became of the Grolf?

I don't know.

What I do know is this: The Grolf is real. And it cannot be stopped. Fortunately (if there is a bright side), it only appears under special circumstances. Unfortunately, in Northern Ontario, those circumstances appear frequently.

So let this be a warning to you. When you're out in the woods, camping, hiking, fishing – whatever – and it starts raining, take notice. If the sun and moon appear, it rains and a rainbow manifests, drop what you're doing and leave. As fast as possible.

The Grolf awaits. And when it feeds, it leaves nothing but the bones.

The Forever Forest

I was playing in the yard with my Tonka truck, alone with my thoughts, as I'd done many times before. I was shy, so the neighbourhood kids didn't like me, and I rarely played sports, which only made things worse. Fortunately, my backyard was connected to a small forest, which provided plenty of diversion for me and my burgeoning imagination.

The grass was moist from the morning's rainfall. The lawn was mucky and gross. Needless to say, I was covered head-to-toe in dirt, as I vroomed my toy truck along the rim of the yard, digging up dirt and rocks and worms. I inched along the sodden soil on shabby knees, truck in hand, heading towards my favourite tree. This tree, a wondrous red oak, stood at the edge of the forest, overlooking our yard. My father had built a ladder going up it, so I could climb it real high. I liked that. Sometimes, I would read books up there until it got dark.

This particular afternoon, however, I didn't feel like climbing. I was having fun gathering acorns and mixing them with the mud and stones, pretending to build a house.

Then I heard a voice.

"Freddie," the voice whispered.

I looked up, startled. No one was there, so I kept playing.

"Psst. Freddie. Over here."

Again, I looked around. Nothing. Although my heart was racing, being ten years old, I was too young to worry. That would come later. So, I shrugged and kept playing. Then my Tonka truck started driving itself. It steered around the base of the red oak, stopping at the tree's other side, that was off the beaten path.

"Ah heck," I scolded, as I crawled to the other side of the tree. I was already filthy. What's more dirt gonna do? Mom makes me wash up before dinner anyways.

The truck beeped, as if telling me to hurry up. By now, I'd forgotten the anonymous voice. I crawled through the foliage, cursing the fallen acorns as they dug into my knees. The truck was parked at the base of the tree, its big black tires clinging to the bark like insects. The tree towered high above me. Its branches, like arms, flexing its might. I looked up and felt nauseous.

The voice came back. "Hey, kid."

There was no one in sight. That's when the fear started creeping in. *I should go home now,* I said to myself.

A heavy gust of wind rustled through my hair.

The tree trembled.

"Nah," the voice replied, sounding like a Bad Guy on TV. "You should stay here. With me."

My truck started flapping its dump bed, as if to agree.

That's when I noticed the face in the tree, staring at me.

"It's more in fun here," the tree said. "You wait and see."

The truck blew its horn, then disappeared into the face of the tree. Anger came quickly. I wanted my truck back. It was a gift from my grandmother.

"Gimme back my truck," I pouted.

The tree huffed and puffed. "C'mon kid. Aren't you the least bit curious?"

I was.

"Then come inside. You'll love it in here. I promise."

The tree was trying to sound pleasant, which only made it worse. I shook my head and crossed my arms.

The tree tittered. Its droopy red eyes were completely insane, its mouth made of bark. My ten-year-old self was both terrified and intrigued. I'd never heard of a talking tree before.

"This can't be real," I told myself.

For a moment, nothing happened. The tree blinked while it waited. Finally, and against my better judgement, I stuck my head inside its elongated mouth. Just for a peak.

The tree swallowed me whole. I felt a WOOSH. Then everything went grey. I don't know how long I was in there for, but when I stepped out, the forest seemed different. The trees loomed larger than life, the air as fresh as a morning sunrise.

"You made it!" a sparrow sang sweetly, before disappearing into the glow of the honeycomb sun.

A red-tailed hawk on a nearby branch, boasted:. "I'm the biggest bird in this forest." Its voice sounded like a chainsaw.

I was dumbfounded. I'd forgotten about my truck.

"Atta boy!" the tree said, scaring me out of my mental slumber. I jumped to my feet with furious fists. I was mad as hell. But also, I was intrigued. Everything around me was bursting with brilliance. The sky was the deepest blue I'd ever seen. The grass as green as a crisp dollar bill.

"Welcome to the Forever Forest," the tree said, grinning ear to ear. It reached out a branch and shook my hand. "You'll love it here, Freddie. I promise."

Words failed me. I was stupefied. My mind was fighting sensory overload. I pinched myself to see if I was dreaming. Turns out I wasn't. Something ran over my foot: my faithful Tonka, which was scooting around in the tall grass, tooting its tiny horn.

"What is this place?" I heard myself ask.

The red oak rustled its branches. "I told you already," the tree said. "You're in the Forever Forest."

I took a tentative step backwards and rubbed my eyes. My truck beeped. A flock of birds were pecking at it, stealing bits from its dump box. The truck raced down the steep incline, letting the birds eat dust.

"Hey! Come back!" I shouted.

My voice ricocheted off the trees like a boomerang. The sound lasted for hours. By now, all eyes were aimed at me, waiting. I stood stupidly in my filthy Spiderman T-shirt, as the red-tailed hawk soared overhead. It scooped up my truck; and before I could protest, it dropped it to my feet.

"Here ya go, kid," the hawk said.

I looked at the toy truck with scorn.

"Toot, toot," said the truck.

Without warning, a deep sadness swept over me. I longed for home. Nothing here seemed real. Yet somehow, I knew it was. I'd discovered a Secret Place., a Land of the Forgotten. A parallel universe, perhaps. Even at my tender age, I knew this meant trouble. Yes, the birds and the trees seemed pleasant, but something in their eyes told me otherwise. They meant to keep me here, forever.

"I wanna go home." I put my foot down as I said this.

The tree rattled in rage. "I'm afraid that's impossible," it said. "Nobody leaves the Forever Forest."

At this moment, the limitations of my age became unbearable. I yearned for an adult to come rescue me.

"Uh-uh," I protested.

The tree shook violently. The ground quivered.

I shot off like a firecracker, screaming down the slope, until my feet became tangled and I tripped. Consequently, I rolled down the hill like a bumbling avalanche. When I reached the bottom, my arms and legs were riddled with scrapes and bruises.

I dropped to my knees and bawled my eyes out. I don't remember being sadder and more scared in my life. My tears formed a river, which flowed freely through the forest, reaching as far as my watering eyes could see.

It was the onset of nightfall that sobered me up. The sun was sinking like a stone. The moon hung overhead, big and round and full. Apparently, time in this world was different. My tummy tossed and turned, reminding me I was famished.

Just then an apple rolled down the hill, stopping at my feet. It was as red as a firetruck, plump as Thanksgiving dinner. I picked it up, dusted it off and took a bite. The apple was delicious. By far, the juiciest apple ever to grace my lips. I ate greedily.

Lightning flashed overhead, casting sinister shadows all around me. Thunder roared its wrongful wrath. I became grossly self-conscious feeling the gaze of the trees, standing over me. I didn't belong here. This much was obvious. I scanned the vicinity. The forest was endless. I was too scared to venture any deeper, so I hurried back up the hill, looking for the face in the tree. Surely, if I asked nicely, it would let me leave.

When I reached the top of the hill, the tree cackled.

"Back so soon, Freddie Boy?"

The neighbouring trees snickered.

I was about to reply, when I felt a drop of rain, followed by another. Suddenly, the world went dark. Rain fell like missiles, soaking me head to toe. I crossed my arms and pouted, getting wetter by the second.

The tree scoffed.

"It's just a little rain, Freddie Boy. You're not scared of rain, are you?"

I shivered. My translucent skin succumbed to the wetness of my grimy clothes. I felt miserable. Without a second thought, I ventured to the front of the tree. Fortunately, Daddy's steps were still nailed into its bark. I climbed up, stopping under a thick branch which provided some much-needed shelter.

"I wanna go home," I said, shaking like the tree leaves.

"You ARE home," the tree replied. "Isn't that right?"

"Why, of course," the surrounding trees responded, in a chorus of agreement.

"But…"

"Just remember kid," the tree interrupted. "Do NOT listen to the snake."

"S-s-snake? What snake?"

The forest erupted with laughter. Every animal, big and small, joined in. And with that, the Forever Forest fell under a blanket of silence. Subtle snoring wafted through the thicket of trees like a lonesome lullaby. I never wanted to be home as badly as I did at that moment.

My mind meandered to my parents. Every terrible thing I'd said to them came flooding back, like a bad dream. Would they even miss me? The other kids in the neighbourhood surely wouldn't. Nobody liked me. Maybe I was better off in the Forever Forest. Maybe I could finally make some real friends. Friends who liked me.

My eyes filled with tears. Fatigue came fast, as I curled up in between two strong branches and drifted into a restless sleep.

...

Something slithered. I awoke in a flash. My screams were a tidal wave of displeasure. The tree shook its leaves, then returned to its peaceful slumber.

"Hello, Fredrick," a slippery voice said. It took a moment for my eyes to adjust. "Don't be alarmed," said the snake. "I'm your friend. Your BEST friend."

A six-foot rattlesnake was weaving its way across my arms and legs. Its skin felt like sandpaper. My fear of snakes was merciless. I froze, not daring to move, besides there was nowhere to go except down. I considered jumping. The fall would hurt, but it wouldn't be lethal. At least, not in the Normal World.

"I wanna go home," I said, embarrassed by my grief-stricken voice.

"Well," said the snake, staring deep into my eyes. "Maybe I can help you with that." It slid up my body, stopping directly in front of my face. The smell of soggy reptile skin steeped into my nostrils.

"Y-you can?" I stuttered.

The snake's large head bobbed.

"Of course!" the snake boasted, eyes sparkling as it spoke. "I'm the ruler of these here parts."

"You are?" I asked. "Then do it. Pleeeeease."

"That will depend on what you're willing to do for me."

There's always a catch. Even as a child I knew this to be true. "What do you want from me?"

The snake hissed. When its forked tongue fondled my nose, my bladder nearly gave out.

"Well," it said surreptitiously. "Let's see what we've got to work with." The snake, now inches from my eyes, was penetrating my mind, rattling around, rummaging through my memories.

"Ah, yes," it said, after an uncomfortable length of time. "You'll do just fine."

By now, I'm as scared as I've ever been. My arms and legs were cramped, and if I didn't relieve my bladder, I'd explode.

A scurry of squirrels gathered at the trunk of the tree, cautiously looking up. The snake backed off a bit. Its dour face produced what I imagined to be a smile.

"Let me introduce myself," said the snake. "The name's Salvador. But folks around here call me Spook."

Spook spoke with the air of royalty. This was no ordinary snake. Heck, this was no ordinary forest. He slithered up an adjacent branch and wrapped himself around it, never taking his eyes off mine.

Without hesitation, I climbed down the tree, found some bushes and peed. It felt glorious.

Spook laughed. "Well done, kid. Well done."

When I finished, I was surprised to see Spoke slinking around my ankles.

"Now," he said, in a more serious tone. "Let's get down to business, shall we?"

We did.

Spook talked. He had plenty to say.

Spook promised to bring me back to my world, no questions asked, but only if I made him famous. I chuckled at the thought, thinking I was getting off easy. There would be consequences, Spook warned, but he assured me they'd be minute. And for my troubles, he added with a wisp, I'd have all the earthly pleasures at my disposal.

Happily, I agreed.

"Excellent," said the snake.

He led me back to the talking tree, where I was surprised by a handwritten contract waiting in the exposed roots. I'd never seen such fancy script before. The paper seemed ancient, like from mediaeval times, and looked to be made of animal skin. Beside the contract, was a fountain pen. I dipped the pen into the bottle of ink next to it.

"Sign on the dotted line," said the snake. "Then you can return to your home. And I shall become famous."

I didn't trust the sound of his voice, nor the look in his beady black eyes, but what choice did I have? I signed the parchment.

The snake smiled.

"I'll see you in your dreams, kid."

Small circles swirled inside Spook's eyes as he spoke, hypnotising me, and I became disoriented. Then everything went dark and I fell asleep.

...

I awoke next to the tree, squint-eyed and confused. I stood up abruptly and fell over. I tripped over my Tonka truck.

"Toot, toot," said the truck.

Fear filled me fast. Was I still in the Forever Forest? Good God, I hoped not.

Up ahead was the edge of the tree line, leading to my backyard. I ran full steam ahead, forgetting my toy truck. There was a commotion coming from inside my house. Something had happened. Something bad. Before I knew it, my grandmother was embracing me. She was weeping.

My mind filled with dread. Something was wrong. Terribly wrong. What had I done?

My grandmother said four words that would forever change the course of my life: "Your parents are dead."

As it turned out, I'd only been gone for a few hours, during which time my parents slipped away to pick up groceries for dinner, while my grandmother waited at home. My parents never returned. How could they? On their way back from the grocery store, they were side-swiped by a transport truck, killing them instantly.

The rest of that summer was a blur. I stayed with my grandmother, who later adopted me. The feeling that I was somehow responsible for my parent's death burned into my brain. My grief helped me forget the Forgotten Forest. I must've fallen asleep beside the tree and dreamed the entire episode. Slowly over time, I convinced myself of this.

All I wanted was my parents to return. They never did, of course. They were dead.

The following school year, my class was assigned to write a story. The best story would be printed in the local newspaper. I dove into this project as though my life depended upon it. Maybe it did. Since the passing of my parents, my classmates resented me even more. Their teasing was relentless. I'd become the Orphan Boy.

This story was all I had.

The story wrote itself. I called it The Adventures of Forever Forest. In it, I included a talking snake named Spook, who ruled over the Forever Forest; and our hero, Chester, a toy truck, who protected the forest creatures from Spook and his inevitable wrath.

The story won first prize, and to my amazement, was published by several prominent magazines across America. Next thing I know, I'm on the news, and Spook is famous. I was eleven years old. This was all new to me.

The Forever Forest was adapted into a popular video game. Cha-ching. My post-secondary was now paid for. My grandmother was over the moon with pride. My good fortune continued. By the time I finished high school, I was the number-one selling author of creepy children's books. Turns out, the world couldn't get enough of the Forever Forest. Millions of children worldwide fell in love with Spook and his slithering setbacks. Chester's adventures were contagious. Twelve books later – including several Pixar adaptations – I'm rich beyond my wildest dreams. That's how I became America's cherished children's author.

My beautiful wife, Isabelle, adored me wholeheartedly. Her love never wavered. She was my rock. My soulmate. My reason for living. For a while, life was grand.

But life isn't about happy endings, is it?

Which leads me to the reason why I'm writing this story in the first place. Something happened to me that curious afternoon. The day I signed my life away to a talking snake in a lively forest. Something peculiar. Not only did I lose both my parents, the two people who truly loved me. I've aged. I look and feel twice my age, on a good day. Which is why I rarely do interviews. Fortunately, my success has awarded me the luxury of shunning myself from the rest of the world. I'm a reclusive author. It's to be expected.

The reason I was able to scribble down so many stories in such a short amount of time is because Spook would narrate them to me in my sleep. Every so often, he'd pay me a visit, and I'd wake up with a bundle of fresh ideas. All I had to do was jot them down. Which I did, to the praise of millions of readers.

Recently however, Spook stopped visiting me. Thus, the stories dried up. To make matters worse, my wonderful wife passed away. Brain cancer. She didn't have a chance. Soon I'll be seeing her. My dreams tell me this. In fact, I'll be gone by the time any of you read this. Even typing these words is a chore. My hands ache. My bones creak. I'm as blind as a bad idea.

My Tonka arrived this morning. I hadn't seen that silly yellow truck since that fateful day in the woods. This is the sign I've been waiting for. Today I shall return to the Forever Forest. It's still there, I can assure you. Only this time I'll be staying. My time has come.

Thank you, Forever Reader, for all you've given me. I've lived a king's life, and I owe it all to you. Well, you and a speaking serpent who goes by the name Spook. And lest we forget, Chester and the talking tree and all the other creatures in the lesser-known land I discovered long ago. Yes, I'm heading back to the source of all the magic. The one place I truly belong: the Forever Forest.

My Christmas Dinner was Worse than Yours

"Get your scrawny ass outta bed, and park it at my dinner table by five o'clock! DON'T be late."

Gramma Benedict is eighty-three and feisty as ever. It's best not to cross her. Especially around the holidays. I sprang outta bed. You see, Benedict Christmas dinners are spectacular disasters. Far worse than yours, I bet.

I do love my Gramma, the old coot, and I especially love her cooking. It sure beats eating Spam out of the can. Although, don't get me wrong, I do make one helluva Christmas Spam.

"Yes Gramma," I groaned. "I'll be there. With bells on."

"That's a good boy, Terry. You always were my favourite, you know." Her voice was as crisp as pie crust. "Don't tell your sister I said that. She's coming as well. In case you didn't already know."

I didn't.

"Okay Gramma. I gotta run, but I'll see you soon. Love you lots."

I ended the call and looked at the mirror. I looked dreadful. Ever since my work was forced to shut down, I've been dwindling away. I made myself a pot of Mac and Cheese for lunch, and to spice it up this time, I added basil and ketchup. Mmm mmm, a true delicacy. At least tonight, Gramma will feed me something that didn't come from a can.

Gramma lives two hours away, in the middle of the boonies, in a lovely old home my Gramps built many years ago. As usual, I was the last one to arrive.

"Oh, look who finally decided to show up," my sister Rachel said, in her Loud Voice; a voice that could wake the dead.

I smiled bitterly, not responding. My big sis was always this way. Gramma came racing over to take my coat, wearing her favourite holiday dress and finest jewellery. Her house was fully decorated, right down to the mistletoe I was unknowingly standing under. Gramma gave me a wet smack on the cheek in front of everyone. I blushed.

Gathered in the living room were my sister, her annoying husband Larry, my cousin Clyde, his latest girlfriend Emma, and of course, his kids Megan and Jayden, both of whom are from Clyde's previous girlfriend Brittany, who inadvertently ran off with the circus. (No, seriously. Her last known whereabouts was Manchester England, where she was setting fire to things then jumping through them in scanty outfits.)

The kids came charging over.

"UNCLE TERRY!" I was plundered, probed and pick-pocketed.

It's difficult to say which kid is worse; my heart tells me Jayden, with his pudgy little hands always covered in goop, but my brain says Megan, with her devilish-red hair, sparkling green eyes and freckles. I swear she could get away with murder. She probably has. Megan and Jayden pulled me into the living room, where everyone had gathered for drinks and hors d'oeuvres.

The fireplace was warm and welcoming; on the mantelpiece hung seven knitted stockings, each filled to the brim with presents. Beside the fireplace was the Christmas tree; it was big and round and festive and smelled of pine needles. Gramma's ashen-white angel topped the tree. She's had it for as long as I can remember. Sadly, the angel has a broken wing. How poetic. It was either Jayden or Megan who broke the angel; each claiming it was the other. This happened the previous Christmas. (Turns out, the little terrors weren't finished with it just yet. But I'll get to that shortly.)

"Where's your date, Terry?" Clyde asked, while sipping on his eggnog, smiling like an asshole. "Surely you didn't come solo,"

Even from where I was standing, he wreaked of rum. He was already intoxicated. Being my least favourite cousin, I ignored him, and found a seat at the end of the couch and tried to get comfortable. Gramma handed me a tall, thick glass of eggnog. I tasted it. It was delicious. There must have been three shots of rum in the drink.

Clyde's question hung in the air, like cigarette smoke. All eyes were on me, waiting for my response.

"Oh, I'm sorry," I said, smartly. "It seems that Plenty of Fish was temporarily out of rent-a-dates. And sadly, my underage mail-order bride will be arriving late this year."

"Zing!" Larry said.

Larry was wearing the ugliest Christmas sweater I'd ever seen. It was puke green and decorated with pink candy canes that clearly looked like penises.

Rachel immediately took charge. She turned down the Christmas music then gave us our instructions: we were to play What Do You Meme? Family Addition. Something told me this was a bad idea.

It was.

Straight away, my sister and her dumbass husband started arguing; like, really arguing. This made the children anxious, so they ran off and started playing. One thing led to another, and one of the little brats knocked over Gramma's tree, breaking several ornaments, including the angel's wing, yet again. That's two years in a row now. A new family tradition.

Rachel scoffed.

"JAYDEN! MEGAN! GET OVER HERE. NOW."

The punk kids ignored her; instead, they rushed around, spilling her eggnog all over Larry's hideous holiday sweater.

"Ugh! Look what your little shitheads did," she said to Clyde, who seemed mildly pleased. Clyde, three years my senior, was an idiot. There, I said it. The guy didn't have a clue. But he somehow made a decent living doing a job which nobody understood; something with computers was all anyone knew. Probably, it was illegal.

Clyde tried calming the kids down. It didn't work of course. They whizzed past him and raced upstairs and started bouncing on Gramma's bed, screaming their bratty little faces off. His barely-legal girlfriend was about to speak up, but he shot her a look. She shut her mouth.

Rachel was scolding both Larry and Clyde, while I helped Gramma with the tree. That's when I noticed Clyde's bottle of tequila. I helped myself to a shot. It was gross, but its affect was instantaneous.

Something was burning in the kitchen.

"Oh, dear me!" Gramma split, only to return a minute later, covered in sweat and grease and turkey guts. "Dinner's ready!"

"More like burned," Rachel said, under her breath.

Larry shook his head and rolled his eyes.

"Don't start with me," Rachel cautioned.

The bird was plump and mouth-watering, as were all the fixings. The smell was scrumptious. We found our spots at the dinner table, eagerly awaiting the feast. The kids seemed unlikely to settle down, chattering away non-stop; the adults were more-than tipsy. Larry tried making a toast, but he was ignored. When he asked me to pass the peas, I was scarfing down my mash potatoes, so I didn't hear him.

Larry asked again, forcefully.

Clyde, who was sitting beside me, took a pea and flung it at him. The children giggled, approvingly. Even Gramma had a good chuckle. Nobody likes old Larry, not even Gramma.

We ate. The booze flowed. The conversations staggered. Arguments ensued. The tequila, along with the bottles of red and white wine, added to the enmity. I watched in fascination as the dinner got more and more aggressive and alarming.

"Larry, don't chew with your mouth open," Rachel ordered. To my surprise (and delight), Larry gave her the middle finger, then began to chew louder.

"Terry, why are you single? Is there something we should know?" Clyde teased, while helping himself to Gramma's famous stuffing.

Gramma intervened. "Clyde, why won't you get back together with Stephanie. She is the mother of your children, for Chrissakes.

"And at least she's old enough to vote." I added.

"Zing."

Clyde's date turned cranberry red.

"Gramma, shouldn't you be in a home by now? I'm worried about you."

"Yikes."

"You're looking awfully thin, Terry."

"We didn't say grace."

"Shut up Larry. You're such a flake!"

"You would know. All you do is boss everyone around. Probably why your own family hates you and your friends talk behind your back."

"Zing."

"Hmmph!"

"I'm not hungry."

"I need to poo!"

"Mommy! Jayden farted at the table!"

"Now, now everyone. Let's try to calm down. We are all here for…"

A blob of mashed potatoes landed on Larry's bald head; it slid slowly down his face.

A hush fell over the table.

Larry, to his credit, took a handful of creamed corn and flicked it at Rachel, who stood up in protest. In doing so, her glass of red wine tipped over and spilled all over her pretty pink dress.

"Now look at what you made me do!"

Things were escalating; I kept eating, trying to avoid danger, but my efforts were in vain. Soon I was wearing Clyde's cranberry sauce. Gramma, God bless her, was laughing heartily. I swear to God I saw her fling a turkey breast at my sister, hitting Rachel square in the face. The children watched in growing fascination. Their eyes lit up like Gramma's Christmas tree.

Jayden took a pile of pudding and dumped it on his sister's head.

"I'm telling," she cried, but no one heard.

War was declared. Game on.

Larry took a swig from the tequila bottle, then spit it all over Rachel.

"You're supposed to swallow, NOT spit," Rachel cried. "You of all people should know this."

"You miserable cunt."

At this point Megan started crying; her face was glowing red.

I stood up, double-fisted, throwing meat and carrots at Clyde. He returned the favour, basting me in turkey broth. To my amazement, Gramma was filming this on her new iPhone. Unfortunately, Gramma slipped and dropped the phone. Jayden, who was dancing on top of the kitchen table, leapt off the table, smashing the phone to pieces.

Gramma got angry.

"You little shit."

She grabbed him by his fatty fingers and flung him over her knee, and started spanking him, old-school style.

"Go Gram!" I shouted, just before getting a glass of red wine dumped over my head.

Rachel and Larry were breaking up right before our eyes. She called him names, that if I put into this story, would land me in a whole heap of trouble. What a shit-show.

Gravy, peas, green beans, salad, turkey slices, buttered bread, stuffing, cranberry sauce, cooked carrots, creamed corn, meatballs, red and white wine, tequila and mashed potatoes were all flying simultaneously across Gramma's hapless dinner table.

I was about to dump the remainder of my plate onto Clyde's head, when I suddenly smelled smoke coming from the kitchen.

"Gramma! You left something on in the kitchen!"

"Oh dear!"

The smoke detector should have sprung to life by now, but hadn't. Turns out, she hadn't replaced the batteries since the Obama days. Gramma disappeared, and came out moments later with a fresh bottle of wine.

Jayden, now in his underpants and using meatballs like cannons, was taking shots at Clyde: *Ping; Ping; Ping.* The little brat was quite the little sniper. There was no stopping him. Clyde sat with his head between his legs, vomiting. This didn't stop Jayden from firing food at him. It was the only time I'd ever seen someone puking while having meatballs pelted onto their head. The smell was alarming. Megan pointed with disgust; she turned green and puked on her plate, adding to the stench.

"STOP IT ALL OF YOU!"

Gramma was going to burst.

We stopped and stared at each other in bewilderment. The dinner table was a disgrace. There was more food on our faces than on our plates. A sad silence fell over the dinner table, as our eyes fell to our plates.

I started laughing. Larry joined in, and soon we were all laughing. We laughed and laughed. The kids were howling, holding their tiny tummies.

Then came the knock on the door.

It was the police.

Clyde tried standing, but he ended up on the floor, passed out in his own puke. In doing so, a candle knocked over. The flame found the puddle of tequila, and Gramma's table burst into flames. Larry dropped his glass of wine – WHOOMP there it is – the drapes caught fire.

The fire spread like Christmas cheer.

Meanwhile, Gramma answered the door. Behind her, the dining room was ablaze, the fire spreading faster than an STD.

A bulging cop stood at the door.

"Everything alright, Ma'am? I was called due to a disturbance." He peaked over her shoulder. "I smell fire."

He barged in.

Before Gramma could answer, the Christmas ham sailed across the room, landing on the cop's head. Next came the meatballs. *PING; PING; PING.*

Gramma looked up and smiled at the ham-covered police officer and puckered her old leathery lips.

"Looks like someone is standing under the mistletoe-toe!"

The Haunted Pub

My first month on the job went without incident. I was hired as head chef, seeing how Raymond, the previous chef, quit unexpectedly. The pub, which was originally built in the late 1700's, then rebuilt in 1823, is located in downtown Ancaster, a quiet village in Southern Ontario. The pub seats roughly sixty people, and boasts live music four nights a week. It's a cozy room, and the food is fantastic, if I do say so myself.

Last week, while delivering a tray of steaming hot glasses to the bar, I saw a ghost.

It was a Sunday, I remember. The pub was dead. Only one table remained; the patrons were finishing their drinks, discussing how they would split the bill. Sitting alone at the end of the bar was a middle-aged woman; she was attractive and well-postured, and wore a broad-brimmed hat and a thin, gauzy white dress. There was a sadness surrounding her. But I was busy working, so I paid her little notice. All I wanted was for this shift to end – and pronto – so I could enjoy a cold, refreshing pint.

Brennagh, the bartender that night, hurried past me, while ignoring the woman sitting at the bar, who was without a drink.

"Um, I think that woman needs a drink," I said to Brennagh. "Or her bill."

I regretted these words as soon as I'd spoken them. Never tell a bartender how to do their job, right? That said, I couldn't figure out why Brennagh, who's a wonderful barkeep, would allow a customer to sit unserved for so long.

Brennagh glanced toward the bar and made a face. "There's no one sitting at the bar," she said, sounding annoyed.

I thought Brennagh was teasing me, as I'm the new guy. But when I checked, the woman in the broad-brimmed hat was gone. I was stunned. I wanted to say something clever, but I was lost for words. Instead, I made a joking gesture, like I was kidding with her, then scampered back to the kitchen where I belonged. When the kitchen was closed and my work completed, I bounced back to the bar, anxiously awaiting my after-work pint. I sat at the bar, drinking my beer. My mind was racing. I couldn't stop thinking about that woman in the broad-brimmed hat. Was she a hallucination? Probably, she was. Weird. Either way, I sat at the opposite end of the bar, just in case. It's a modest sized bar, so I was still within spitting distance of where the woman was sitting.

I finished my beer, and soon forgot about the mysterious woman. I was ready for home. As I was putting on my coat and scarf, bracing for the icy weather waiting for me outside, the woman appeared in the corner of my eye.

"Gotcha!" I snapped, looking across the bar to where she was sitting. She vanished. I rubbed my eyes and shook my head. I must be losing it, I thought, unhappily. Maybe it was stress.

Wearily, I left for home. I couldn't get the woman in the broad-brimmed hat out of my head. Was she real, or was my mind playing tricks on me? Maybe this was some elaborate prank the staff were playing on me. Could be, but that was highly unlikely. Maybe I really was losing it. I mean, cooking is stressful…

When I returned to work a couple nights later, I felt better. It was Trivia Night, which meant the pub would be packed. Work was beyond strenuous; the kitchen, hot enough to scald a loon, looked more like a war zone than a place to prepare food.

Sometime after eight o'clock, when it finally died down a bit, I took my dinner break. I sat at the edge of the bar, eating my burger in silence. I was famished. As I was dipping my French fries into a giant glob of ketchup, lost in my thoughts, I spotted the woman in the broad-brimmed hat; she was sitting at the bar, next to a group of large men, who were drinking and roaring and having the time of their lives. This woman, on the other hand, remained eerily quiet. It was like she wanted to go unnoticed.

As Brennagh whizzed past me, I motioned to the woman sitting at the end of the bar. "What now?" Brennagh shot me a nasty look. It was obvious she didn't like me. Maybe because I was filthy and smelled like fish bait. "You're pointing to the only spot no one's sitting in. You do know this, right?"

"Huh?"

When I peaked past the men drinking at the bar, the mysterious woman was gone. I gasped. Brennagh, on the other hand, muttered some choice words under her breath, then scooted off to serve some drinks.

I was too frightened to even so much as glance across the bar, where up until a moment ago, the woman wearing the brimmed-brimmed hat was seated. But if she wasn't really sitting there, then how come her bar stool remained vacant? This was peculiar, because the pub was jam-packed. Every table and chair were filled except hers. It was as if some unknown force was preventing people from sitting there. This made zero sense.

My hands were shaking. Nothing made sense to me anymore. As I was heading back to the kitchen, I felt a pair of eyes following me. I knew who it was. It was the woman sitting at the bar. When I glanced over my shoulder, she was back, sitting at the end of the bar. Tentatively, I took a step toward her, then she disappeared again. Poof. Just like that. She was gone. Resisting the urge to scream, I scooted back to the kitchen, not looking back.

As impassively as possible, I asked Dave, the line-cook working with me that night, about the haunted history of the pub. I'd heard rumours of such, but chalked them up to folklore. Dave ignored me; instead, he put five pounds of chicken wings into the deep fryer and pulled out a tray of nachos from the oven.

I asked him again. Dave remained silent for an unusual length of time; eventually, he looked up from the plate of nachos he was dressing and scrutinised me.

"Are you serious?" he asked. "Or just being a jerk?"

Not the response I was expecting. When I mentioned the woman sitting at the bar, his eyes lit up.

"You've seen her?" He was unable to contain his excitement. "Wicked! I've only heard of her."

Dave pulled the wings from the deep fryer, shook off the grease, applied the appropriate sauces, then plated them. I rang the bell, and the server quickly came to retrieve them. We got slammed. The subject didn't come up again until later that night, after work.

I bought Dave an after-work pint, he guzzled with glee. Then I ordered another round. I wanted to loosen his lips. Dave's worked here for years. If anyone knows something, it's him.

"She was sitting right there." I pointed to the stool at the end of the bar, next to the warmly-decorated fireplace with the rose-coloured stockings hanging from the mantel.

Dave peeked over my shoulder; smiled nervously, then leaned in close and whispered, "Have you been to the basement?"

I shook my head.

The basement is where we store kegs and random cleaning supplies. It's where junk goes to die.

The next round of drinks arrived. We cheersed.

Dave took a generous gulp, wiped his mouth on the sleeve of his Metallica t-shirt. Then he looked me dead in the eyes.

"The pub is haunted," he said, just above a whisper. "And has been for as long as anyone can remember. Personally, I haven't seen any ghosts, but Ray told me stories. Creepy stories, which included this lady you're describing."

Dave paused to slurp his beer, then belched. "Ray hated this place. Especially the basement. Probably why he quit." He shot me a strange look. "You know the town's history, don't you?"

I didn't.

"The town of Ancaster is old. Well, old for this part of the world. Across the street is where they kept the gallows. That's where they hanged war criminals, traitors, and your run-of-the-mill ruffians. They hanged a lot of men during the War of 1812. And were ruthless about it.

"Did you know that the bloodiest sentence ever handed down – to this day – happened here? They executed fifteen men, all of whom were charged for treason."

I gasped.

Dave's eyes lit up.

"It gets better. These same prisoners resided right here in this very building, waiting for those nasty nooses to snap their necks like twigs."

We drank.

"The most dangerous men were detained in the basement, where they were tortured and tormented. And God knows what else. No wonder the place is haunted. I've been down there. It's super creepy. The floor is grey dirt, the walls are dark and dingy. Plus, it smells musty and old."

Dave's words filled me with dread. I was trying to wrap my mind around what Dave just told me. More beer was required. We waited in silence until the beer arrived.

It was around this time I spotted the woman sitting at the end of the bar. She was facing me. Her skin was a blanket of fresh snow, her eyes crackling with life. My stomach filled with butterflies. Why didn't Dave see her?

"There must be a record somewhere that shows the total number of prisoners executed here," Dave said. "Whatever it is, I'm sure it's a helluva lot. Maybe that's why this pub is haunted."

I pondered this for a moment. It wasn't easy. Until a few days ago, the idea of ghosts seemed ludicrous. In fact, I've made fun of people for believing such hogwash. Now look at me. I'm discussing the ghosts of dead prisoners, while being watched by an apparition only I can see. I stole another glance over my shoulder. The woman was indeed watching me.

Dave looked at me curiously. "She's back, isn't she?"

I nodded. It took all my energy not to completely freak out. Dave turned to face the empty bar stool, where the ghost-woman was sitting, and stared for an incredible length of time. He was squinting. "Dammit," he said. "I see nothing. But I do feel something strange coming over me. Probably my imagination."

He finished his last swallow of ale; then he started gathering his things. His face was as pale as the beer. He thanked me for the beer, said goodbye to Brennagh, then split.

The next day, Dave quit.

By now I had a decent beer buzz, which under normal circumstances would've been great. But not on this particular evening. I was downright spooked. The ghost-woman was scrutinising me with her dour, dead eyes. She rarely moved, just stared. I needed to split – and fast – before my mind collapsed, so I gathered my belongings as quickly as I could, while ignoring the ghost in the broad-brimmed hat.

As I was about to leave the pub, Brennagh came rushing over. "Tony, can you please go down to the basement and bring back a keg of Canadian?" She was flustered, still waiting on a large table, who seemed hellbent on partying all night.

Suddenly, I was trembling like an earthquake. The last thing I wanted to do was venture down the basement, not after what Dave told me. But I did it anyway. What choice did I have?

The stairwell leading down to the basement was narrow. I'm tall, so I had to crouch to avoid knocking my head. I went slowly and cautiously down the wobbly, wooden stairs, trying my best to be brave. It wasn't working. I was scared shitless.

The basement was poorly lit, the air thick and moist. It smelled like mould, plus something else I can't quite describe. If haunted had an odour, this would be it. A discarded beer sign lay in twisted ruins at the bottom of the stairs; stacks of cardboard boxes lined the stone-brick walls, the colour of dead fish.

As I reached the bottom step, I tripped over a dead rat, causing me to whack my head on the edge of the ceiling. It really hurt. I kicked the rat carcass across the room, rubbing my aching head. At the opposite end of the basement, soiled in silvery spiderwebs, was a filthy mop bucket. Next to it was a rusted meat slicer that must be forty years old, at least. Straight ahead of me, leaning haphazardly against the wall, were the kegs.

I found a keg labelled Canadian; I bent down and carefully picked it up, trying not to whack my head on the low ceiling again. As I stood at the base of the stairs, ready to return to the main floor, I felt a cool breeze brush against my face. The basement lights started flickering on and off in sudden flashes.

I checked over my shoulder. Someone rushed past me.

Then came a garbling noise. I dropped the keg on my big toe, crushing it. The keg clanked and clacked and crawled along the grimy basement floor, before coming to an abrupt halt.

My anxiety was skyrocketing. After dropping an inflammatory F-Bomb, I scanned the vicinity, searching for whoever was down here with me. That's when I felt something touch the back of my neck. I spun around in surprise. No one was there. By now, my heart was threatening to explode from my chest; and even though the temperature in the basement was frigid, I was sweating buckets. The walls were closing in. Quickly, I was becoming claustrophobic.

I took a deep breath and held it for six seconds, trying to regain some composure. Then I let out a nervous laugh, and started ascending the stairs. That's when I heard a voice cry out for help. This put a jump to my step. I was halfway up the stairs before I realised I'd forgotten the keg. Cursing my stupidity, I scampered back down the stairs to get the damn keg. That's when I heard the voice again. Fear paralysed me. My legs refused to move. I just stood there, waiting for whatever was down here to show themselves. I knew this was a bad idea, but I couldn't help myself.

Someone was sobbing. The sound was close. I turned my attention to the spandrel behind the stairwell, and saw the most extraordinary site. I gazed, mouth ajar, stone-cold petrified. What I saw has forever altered my perception of reality. I'm still trying to come to grips with it. Maybe that's what's compelling me to share this story. Make it official, so to speak.

As I crept toward the stairwell, a group of gaunt-looking men were huddled together in the cubbyhole behind the stairs. They were chained to the wall, clad in wretched rags, which matched their filthy, malnourished faces. I knew they weren't real, because they were shimmering, like a mirage in the desert; yet, there they were, right in front of me. This broke my heart. I don't care what these men did, this was simply inhumane. I squinted, hoping to get a better look at them. The men were neck to neck, grunting and groaning; one man was weeping profusely, his head buried in his bloodied, soiled hands. Then came the bullwhips cracking, followed by a chorus of screams. I let out a pathetic whimper; and when I did, the men dissolved into thin air.

I rushed to the bottom of the stairs, looking up at the speck of light peeking from behind the entrance, then I began my journey up the slender stairwell. The scene played out again: bullwhips cracking, followed by tortured pleas for mercy.

I nearly leapt out of my skin. With the keg snug in my arms, I ran upstairs and slammed the basement door shut, once and for all. The urge to break down and cry was tremendous. I'd never been so scared in my life. When I delivered the keg to Brennagh, she looked at me peculiarly.

"Jeez," she said. "You look like you've seen a ghost."

I let out one low laugh, then scrambled for my belongings and bee-lined for the exit. As I was leaving, something compelled me to stop and turn around. It was past closing time. The pub was still and silent. Chairs sat on table tops, ready for their nightly slumber; bar stools rested, empty and taciturn. All except one.

The woman in the broad-brimmed hat sitting at the end of the bar appeared. She was looking straight at me. The corners of her lips raised in what could've been a smile. For a moment I simply regarded her; her auburn hair spilled from her eloquent hat, her eyes like black pearls.

I waved goodbye as I left.

To my amazement, she returned the wave.

That night, I dreamt of the dead. The following morning, I sent this email to Rachel, the owner of the Coach and Lantern:

Dear Rachel,

Although my time at the Coach and Lantern has been short-lived, it's been both enjoyable and educational. You run a fine pub. That said, I hereby give you my two-weeks notice. Although I'm grateful for the opportunity you provided me, I feel it's time for a career change. I want to write horror stories. Yes, it's time I write about ghosts and haunted houses and evil spirits and such. Sounds like fun, right? One last thing: I won't be venturing into the basement again. Ever.

Best of luck to you and your pub,

Tony Styles

Monster Street

I was walking home from school when it happened, daydreaming away. I must've taken a wrong turn. It was late February. The dead of winter. The menacing wind was blowing me backwards, as I trudged through the cold sleet and snow.

I turned onto what should've been my street, thinking nothing of it. Something seemed wrong with the street – I'd be lying if I said otherwise – but I was nine. My only concern was to wrap my hands around my Nintendo controller, cozy up on the couch, and get lost in the wonderful world of Zelda.

The wind abruptly stopped.

Without the insistent chatter of wind fighting my frost-bitten face, I was able to see further ahead. What first caught my attention – more like raised the tiny hairs on my prepubescent arms – was the houses. They were watching me. Callous whispers mocking me as I tramped across the icy sidewalk.

I kept walking. A car pulled up. A classic Roadster from the 1930's. The car reminded me of my big sister's ZZ Top record, Eliminator.

The driver got out and waved.

That's when I knew I was in trouble.

The man – and I use this term loosely – was easily seven feet tall and slim as a pole. He wore a pinstripe, double-breasted suit and matching fedora, and enough jewellery to satisfy any hip hop artist. His muscular face was finely chiselled. My stomach tightened at the very sight of him. This was a Bad Man.

I returned the wave and kept walking, stealing sideways glances to make sure he wasn't sneaking up on me. He wasn't. Nope, he glided effortlessly toward his picturesque suburban home and morphed into it. His feet never touched the ground.

I picked up the pace. It still hadn't dawned on me yet that this wasn't my street. Another car pulled up. It looked like the car from Scarface, which my sister made me watch, against my will.

I put my head down and kept walking, fast as I could.

The car honked at me, AROOOGAH!.

I didn't dare look back.

The driver shouted, "Hey Kid!" in a voice so gruff it would make the Marlboro Man quit his job.

I bolted.

I ran flat out until I reached the end of what should've been Sanderson Drive – my street – and was greeted by the bone-chilling wind and the sudden onslaught of darkness. My heart was a Jack-in-the-Box, ready to evacuate.

I stood frozen in fear for quite some time, until my mother drove up, saving me. I jump inside the car, bringing with me a bucket of tears and no clear answers to her plethora of questions. Apparently, I'd been gone for hours. I tried telling her about the Bad Man, but it all came out as gibberish.

…

Days went by and life moved on. The memories of that Bad Man and his mobster-mobile faded into oblivion. That is until four years later.

It's February 29, 1992, the day was drab and dreary. By now, I'm thirteen and chalk-full of teenage insolence. I'm walking home from school with Nirvana blasting on my CD Walkman. Unbeknownst to me, the street of monsters had returned.

The Roadster rolled up next to me, letting the car idle its ugly roar. The driver waved me over. Memories of my scared nine-year-old self returned like a bad rerun. This was the same man as before: The Bad Man.

"Ain't ya gonna wave back?" the monster-man asked. His voice sounded like machine gun fire.

I shook my head, avoiding his terrible gaze.

He stepped out of the car and approached. His rusted lips twisted into a scowl. Before I knew it, he was towering over me, seething. By thirteen, I was quite tall, but nowhere near as tall as this well-tailored creep. When he touched my shoulder, a million screams of terror trampled across my soul. My legs buckled, I collapsed.

Another roadster pulled up. Four men wearing matching garments spilled out, standing tall as mountains. Their faces were ugly. These were Bad Men. And they meant harm. They moved effortlessly my way, grinning like gamblers.

Meanwhile, the Bad Man dragged me to my feet. He nestled his bony fingers into my shoulder blade and pressed down hard. The pain was egregious. Without a second thought, I kicked my boot down on its foot with the full force of fear. Then I booked it.

While running, I noticed the peculiarity of the houses. They were alive, and regarding me as one might watch a sporting event. In fact, they were betting on whether or not I'd come out alive.

"You'll never make it, you nincompoop," a beige bungalow said in a smoky voice. A chorus of agreement followed.

The Bad Men were gaining on me. Probably, they were toying with me, getting my hopes up, before killing me. The houses cheered them on as they chased me. I ran as fast as any teenage boy can, faster maybe. Fortunately, I made it off the street. Right back where I started. Something didn't add up. I turned around, expecting to see the thugs, but my proper street appeared out of thin air. Wasting little time, I hightailed home and crawled into bed and didn't come out until the following morning.

The next morning, I noticed the claw marks covering my badly bruised shoulder. Soon enough, those marks were discovered by my parents, who rushed me to the hospital. Nothing came of it. But those marks lasted all summer. I thought they'd never go away.

Sometime later, I told my best friend Michael about the street of monsters. Naturally, he thought I was lying. Micheal started spreading rumours about me, which resulted in terrible teases and name-calling. Needless to say, I never told another soul about that nefarious street of mobster-clad ghouls. From then on, I kept the street of monsters a secret.

I was with my high school sweetheart the next time the street appeared. Four years later, to the day. We'd just gotten off the city bus and turned onto my street, eager for some alone time before my parents got home.

Once again, I'd forgotten about the street of monsters. Likewise, I'd forgotten it was a leap year, although I hadn't made that connection yet. These things didn't mean much to my seventeen-year-old self.

We'd had a record-setting snowfall that week. My town was buried under a mountain of snow. It was difficult to see your hand in front of your face, let alone some strange street with talking houses, and bad guys who drove cool cars and floated across the snow as they walked. But as soon as the vintage car pulled up, everything came flooding back. That's when I made the connection: Leap Year. How could I be so stupid?

Then I freaked out.

"Run!" I said, grasping Trisha's tiny hands under her brightly-coloured mittens.

Trish chuckled, thinking I was being cute.

I wasn't.

"Hey!" the monster shouted in a bullet-ridden voice. Dressed to the nines, he stepped out of the vehicle and lunged toward us, his finely-polished boots never touching the snow.

My girlfriend fainted.

"Trish!" I shouted, desperately trying to lift her. But instead, I slipped and fell flat on my face.

"Gotcha!"

We were yanked to our feet.

The Bad Man held us in a tight grip. I didn't trust the way he was looking at my girlfriend.

Two more Roadsters pulled up and a team of tall men surrounded us. They were all impeccably dressed. Their faces smeared with scorn. The amazing part was how the snow seemed to pass through them, like holograms.

Despite my futile attempts at stopping them, the Bad Men abducted my girlfriend. I watched in horror as they stuffed her into the back of the old Ford. The trunk slammed like a chrome casket. The monsters sped away, vanishing under furious fumes of carbonated clouds.

I was left alone.

Shivering, I called out her name. My voice fell flat onto the nearest snowbank. It was only time before the Bad Men returned. I had to do something.

The street was a morgue. I tried turning around, but in doing so, the street spun with me, making me nauseous. Apparently, there was only one way to go: straight. This can't be real. Everything about this street felt wrong. If only I'd fought harder. I could've prevented those tough guys from taking my girlfriend. Tears froze to my pale and pimpled face like ice on a rink.

A low murmur was coming from the houses. They were mocking me. Garage doors opened and closed, chuckling away; mailboxes flipped their lids, heckling me, while I slump-shouldered my way off this nefarious street.

I fully expected my girlfriend to be waiting for me.

She wasn't.

I sulked home solemnly, wondering what my next move should be. Trisha's parents hated me as it was. They thought I was a 'bad influence' on her. When she failed to return home, things got ugly. Her father swore up and down he would have me killed, but not before maiming and torturing me first. Even my own parents were suspicious.

I spent the following year under constant police surveillance. I won't get into the details because, even to this day, it's too traumatising. Everyone in town believed I murdered my girlfriend and hid her body somewhere. And why not? I was the last known person she was with.

I'd tried explaining the street of monsters, but of course, no one believed a word. Whenever someone searched for it, the street wasn't there. Apparently, Monster Street only appears on February 29 somewhere between 2-3pm. And only to those unfortunate enough to wonder through it.

Makes me wonder how many other kids have gone missing on this day.

I don't remember much of what came next. My mind melted into a cocktail of Antipsychotic drugs. My parents never looked at me the same since. Hell, they still don't. My life was ruined in every way.

All along, I kept thinking Trisha would return. But she never did. After high school, I left that scandalous town and never looked back. Trisha's body was never found.

. . .

I've recently moved back to that innocuous town. And as luck would have it, I bought a house in my old neighbourhood. My job offered me a sweet deal on the place. One I couldn't pass up. I knew this wasn't a coincidence. My past was catching up with me. But my rational mind convinced me otherwise. I'm an adult. There must be a reasonable explanation for what happened so long ago. Whatever it may be.

Which leads me to February 29, 2020. On the cusp of a major pandemic no less. The day was cold and stark. I was walking my dog Capone. After the bullmastiff did his business, we passed my old street. That's when Capone started growling.

Those terrifying childhood memories started nagging the outer limits of my mind, ready to escape if I let them. Stupidly, I rejected those warnings. We turned down Sanderson Drive. I even checked the street sign, just to be sure. Then I sighed. Everything was okay. Obviously. Monster streets don't exist. Not when you're an adult.

Capone led the way.

As I was studying the houses, checking their authenticity, a car pulled up. I recognized it straight away. It was that old Ford Model A. It still looked shiny and new.

When the driver's window rolled down, the Bad Man leaned out and waved. His stone-black eyes stabbed me with knives.

My dog was unusually cautious, his tail glued between his stubby legs. The Bad Man got out of the car and glided effortlessly toward me, his feet inches above the snow-covered ground.

This isn't real. I told myself. No fucking way. But it felt real. Real as the grotesque grin stamped across that ugly monster's face.

Capone went haywire.

I let go of his leash.

He charged. To my surprise, the monster's face recoiled. The thing flew towards the house and morphed into it. The house belched, and then told us to bugger off.

You had to see it to believe it.

"Let's get outta here, old buddy," I said, after giving him a good ol' pet.

Capone pulled me with the sheer force of a strong dog. My jelly-filled legs did their best to keep up. Meanwhile, the row of houses kept slandering us, puffing smoke from their cigar-like chimneys, as we made our escape. We approached the end of Monster Street. A band of mobsters were watching from their front porches; they raised their crooked middle fingers, then disappeared into their houses. The wind began to howl as the normal world returned.

The glow of the fingernail moon hung like an ugly painting. How did it get so dark? Many hours had passed. I was turning away, when I heard a familiar voice coming from the Roadster parked at the edge of that disreputable street. Someone was inside, trying to get out.

"Should we go back?" I asked my pooch.

Capone barked and wagged his tail, looking up with eager eyes. I'd never entered the street from this end before. This may end badly. I feared the worst.

I took one step forward, then Capone shot out of my hands like a flash of white lightning. When I caught up with him, I juddered. Someone was locked in the trunk of the car.

A girl.

"Um, hello?"

"Tommy!" the girl shouted. The sheer terror in her voice was crippling. "Tommy? Is that you?"

"Trish?" I stuttered, through chattering teeth.

"Help me Tommy," the voice pleaded. "Pleeeeease."

Part of me died right there. I simply couldn't believe it. Twenty years of guilt lifted from my shoulders, and landed on the snow with a thud.

"Trish!" I said. "Is it really you?"

"Help me, Tommy. Before the Bad Men come back."

My mind split into a million pieces. I didn't know what to do next.

A shiny set of keys was dangling from the ignition. Nervously, I reached for the door handle, leaned in and swiped the keys, careful not to touch the blameless leather seat, which wreaked of formaldehyde.

Keys in hand, I hustled back to the trunk.

"Tommy, is that you?" The voice inside the trunk asked. Something in her voice sounded off.

The trunk dared me to open it. Shakily, I turned the gold-coloured key. A plume of steam wafted as the apartment-sized trunk swung open like a chrome casket. Inside was a fresh-looking teenage girl with strawberry blond hair with smooth curls folded over her finely-freckled face. Her clothes were in disarray.

"Trish!"

"Help me, Tommy. Pleeeeeease!"

Her hands and feet were shackled.

"Hold on," I said, pacing the street. I needed time to think.

The houses trembled as their doors swung open. The monsters got out, each impeccably dressed. They grunted, then attacked.

I looked down at Trish, whose eyes were big as oceans. Without a second thought, I reached in and pulled her out. Her skin was a block of ice. She weighed a tonne. That didn't stop me. By the time I placed her shackled body onto the sidewalk, I was surrounded by monsters.

"We've been waiting for you, Tommy," the Bad Man said.

The creep soared toward me. In its hand was a straight razor, which glistened under the pale light of the cold street lamp.

When I looked down at Trisha, her eyes turned into X's. My nightmares had come true: She was one of them. She snarled; then she broke apart the chains as if they were straw.

"Come stay with us," the monster who once was my girlfriend said.

"You're not Trish," I managed to say, trying to avoid her X-riddled eyes.

"Oh, but I am," the thing proclaimed, licking its lizardly lips. "And I'm soooo happy here. You will be too. You've been chosen."

Her eyes locked into mine, and I surrendered. I would be happy here, as long as I was with her. Our hands met. She pulled me close and kissed me sweetly. Her lips were linoleum. Suddenly, I was home. The monsters applauded, the houses opened and shut their doors in celebration.

Another car pulled up. The door swung open.

"Get in." The driver said, his fedora shielding his face.

"Okay," I said, in a daze.

"Oh Tommy," Trish said, squeezing my hands. "I just knew you'd come back."

She got in first, then tapped the spot next to her.

I went.

As I was entering the vehicle something grabbed me from behind.

Capone.

The bull mastiff's jaws found the seat of my pants, as he forced me out of the vehicle just in time. I took one last look at my high school sweetheart; her freckled face pouted fiercely, as the X's swam circles in her big blue eyes.

"Let's go, Boy," I said, gripping his leash with both hands.

The monsters protested. Cars honked and sirens rang. Capone led us to safety. When I turned around, the street was gone. No trace of it anywhere. I pulled my phone from my coat pocket and gasped.

"What the…"

It was nine o'clock, which was weird, but to be expected. Time is different on Monster Street. What disturbed me was the date: March 1, 2022.

…

Apparently, I've been missing for two years. My house has been sold, and my position at the firm replaced. My parents are both dead, natural causes. My sister won't talk to me. I have nothing.

Well, not true. I still have Capone; aka the Best Dog Ever. And after much negotiating, I've managed to reacquire some of my assets. Consequently, I'm residing at a cheap motel, contemplating the mess that has become my life. But don't worry about me. I'm a survivor. So is Capone.

May this be a lesson to you: Leap year is fast approaching. On February 29, 2024, you'd best beware. Stay inside. Lock the doors. You wouldn't want to stumble onto Monster Street.

Red Pill

"Go ahead, Ronny. Take it."

That's all it took.

Five words that would forever change the course of my life. What happened after I took Omar's red pill was absolutely terrifying. It still is. I'm still under its affect.

The drug took an hour to kick in.

Then…liftoff.

Something grabs hold of me and starts dragging me backwards. All at once, I'm plunged into the bowels of my mind, like a toilet flushing a turd. Resistance is futile.

Everything stops.

My life is beginning again; gaining speed. But in reverse.

How I forgot to take out the trash, making mother mad.

My first kiss.

My first goal scored in hockey.

My first day of kindergarten. Oh, how I was scared.

I don't know how much more I can take. It's like watching a movie from the end. Except, this isn't a movie. This is my life. And I'm the main character! Every embarrassing moment of my short-lived life is being revisited, most of which I'd forgotten.

I visit Maynard, my childhood friend, the day he falls off his bicycle and gets run over by a bus. I try to stop this tragic event from happening, but cannot. Again, Mayard dies.

And thus my backwards journey continues.

I watch myself grow younger and younger. Each memory is like a dagger to the brain.

I'm flailing and crying as an angry infant, frustrated and confused.

I brace myself, certain of what's coming next:

Helplessly, I watch myself being born.

"Make it stop!" I shout at the top of my lungs, but I have no voice. How could I? I'm passing through a birthing canal. My tiny eggshell brain being crushed, as it passes through a small hole.

Then, I disappear.

And everything changes.

ZAP!

Clouds.

Nirvana.

Alas! I'm in heaven.

"Am I dead?"

I watch in awe as these words fall from my face, like words typed on a screen.

No, I can't be.

I'm in the Void. The barto.

Now I'm ten-feet tall.

I'm omniscient.

In a City of Clouds.

A large sum of time passes; eventually this peaceful, easy feeling turns to dust. And then everything goes dark.

Terror grips what's left of my soul.

I have no body.

I have no name.

Nothing is real.

Nothing to get hung about.

ZAP!

I'm being born again. The pain is unreal.

It's over! Phew. Only now, I'm barefoot and partially clothed, cold as a wet basement.

I'm confused. There are voices, but I don't understand the words.

I'm in a cave.

People are coming.

Soldiers.

They're close!

I start crawling up the wall, trying to escape.

Oh no. They've found me! They're beating me with clubs and spears, blood leaking from every orifice of my measly body.

Helpless and scared, I close my eyes.

Without warning, I'm being whisked backwards, accelerating at incomprehensible speeds.

My life continues its backwards trajectory, rewinding faster and faster, shattering my equilibrium in the process.

Please. Make this stop. My mind is going to crack. Maybe it already has.

ZAP!

My body is covered in thick, matted fur. I stink like faeces.

I'm an animal, killing some hapless beast with brute force, clawing, ripping it to shreds. Then I eat the animal raw, leaving nothing but its bones.

I roar, revelling in my might.

Then moments later, I'm eradicated by a pack of wild boars.

ZAP!

Darkness arrives like an old friend.

I'm in a cage, panting. Scared and claustrophobic. The stench of death is everywhere.

Oh no! I'm in a slaughterhouse. The Man is poking me, shuffling me into the back of a truck. With others. The truck stops. A different Man forces us into a giant silver box.

On a treadmill.

The sweet smell of death.

I'm freaking out.

Blood everywhere.

I see the blade, then nothing.

My death is merciless.

ZAP!

Clarity.

I remember.

Drugs!

I'm on drugs.

I'm gonna kill Omar when I finally wake up. I wonder where he is.

"Omar!" I shout, but I still haven't found my voice.

I'm lost in the Void. Stuck in the In-Between world.

Out of the darkness comes a flickering flame.

It's blood-red, and getting warmer.

Scolding.

I'm in a lake of fire.

Furious flames flash before my eyes. The stench of burning flesh pervades me. My hands are scolding. My eyes are ablaze. I'm chained to a fiery wall. Some unholy creature with horns on his head and razor blades for hands is jabbing sharp and shiny objects into my eyes. Again, and again. The pain is insufferable. My blood-soaked tears burn holes in my scolding cheeks. Meanwhile, my lips are peeled off, then returned, then peeled off again, like someone eating an orange.

This goes on and on, like a cycle of never-ending nightmares. After an eternity of suffering, my shackles are removed.

A small blue door appears.

I lunge towards the blue door like a dog chasing a ball.

The door is open!

There's a tunnel. It's bright.

I pass through the bright tunnel.

ZAP!

I'm outside.

Outside of Mommy.

Wrapped into a warm blanket.

I'm me again!

Only, I'm a newborn, wrinkly and fresh. My father is looking lovingly at me. Next to him is a doctor, who's saying something I don't understand.

I cry myself to sleep.

When I wake up, I'm still in the hospital.

I'm still a baby.

Then I remember:

The Red Pill.

I'm on drugs.

Damn you, Omar. When will this wear off?

Soon, I hope.

I'm trapped, scared, alone. Weeks become months and then become years. Everything's a blur, until my seventh birthday and reality rears its ugly head: I'm reliving my life all over again.

...

That's exactly what happened. Only now, time is moving faster at roughly 1.75x the speed of normal life. A year feels like a month, a day seems like hours. Unfortunately, I cannot change or redo anything. I simply observe, like a guest within its own mind.

I watch my parents slowly drift apart, year after year, until their inevitable breakup. My parents divorced because of me. It's obvious now. They never had any Alone Time. I was always interrupting them with my juvenile problems. The truth stings.

Day by day, year by year, my life again unfolds until twenty-one years finally pass. Time slows down. I'm regaining control. I've finally caught up. You see, today is the Big Day: the day I take Omar's red pill. I've dreamt this day for so long!

Thus lies the paradox.

Do I:

A. Take the red pill (again?) and hope everything returns to normal; thus, having caught up with my life's continuum?

Or:

B. Don't take the pill, play it safe, thus changing history.

My mind is running circles around itself. If I chose A, then I risk falling into the "Groundhog Day" scenario, where I'm trapped reliving the same horrific events over and over again.

On the other hand, if I chose B, and I don't take the drug, I'll be tampering with the very fabric of reality. Because, if memory serves, I did take the red pill. That's what got me in this mess in the first place.

I don't know what the retributions are for altering the course of history, but something tells me there's a heavy price to be paid. My mind is telling me to take the pill and hope for the best; my heart, on the other hand, is opting for option B. If I take Omar's drug, I'll have to relive its awful affects. And I don't want that. In fact, I'm never taking drugs again. Period. Hell, I don't even know what it was I took. Stupid Omar.

Something startled me back to reality: my phone is vibrating. I got a text. It's from Omar. He's telling me to go over to his place. Pronto. He's got something for me.

My hands are trembling as I type this.

Without realising it, I sent my response: C U soon!

I'm on my way to Omar's place. Apparently, his parents are away for the weekend. He says he's discovered this crazy new drug. He wants me to try it.

I've got nothing planned for this evening. Maybe I should go over to Omar's. See what happens. I've already got my boots on. Adios amigos.

I'll let you know how it goes…

The World Is Run By Monsters

The world is run by monsters. They're everywhere. My Grade One teacher was one. The other kids didn't notice that Mrs. DeRosa had long, spider-webbed fingers that turned into claws when she became angry; that her hair was of no actual color and her eyes were empty spaces in the middle of her ginormous head. Or that she was always hungry. But I did.

Then there was my babysitter Ruth, who liked to lick my nose, bite my tongue, and eat green Jell-o by the barrelful. Her eyes were strangely dark; her skin a sickly grey. My parents thought I was crazy. Maybe I was. The doctors sure thought so.

Turns out, I was correct.

Monsters are cunning. They hide in plain sight. And they feed off children. Thus, I learned to keep my mouth shut. If I don't bother them, I figured, maybe they'll leave me alone, and not hurt me. Seemed logical. And hey, at least my parents were normal. If they were monsters, I would have known, right?

When I was age thirteen. I was obsessed with computer programming, diving head first into it, learning as much as humanly possible. It paid off. Now, as an adult, I'm an IT guy, and in high demand. Need help sorting out your pesky computer problems? Call me, I'm an expert. To be honest (I'm not bragging or anything), but over the years I've proven to be the best in the biz. And as they say: business is good.

Over the years, I've kept my ears to the ground, searching for the origin of the monsters. They must come from somewhere, right? Nothing substantial came of my quest; ultimately, I grew tired of monsters. But that didn't stop me from seeing them.

Last month, Washington DC commissioned me to 'spruce up' some highly confidential documents, and 'fix' a laptop that's been a problerm. They wouldn't identify themselves, nor was I permitted to work remotely. They wanted to watch over me. Whoever they are. Naturally, I was suspicious, but work is work, so I took the job. Big mistake. They're watching me, likely reading this as I type. But that's no longer a concern. There are bigger problems. What I found on those laptops is keeping me up at night. Truth be told, I'm terrified. Something needs to be done. But I must be discreet. After what I've discovered, I cannot divulge their names. I may see monsters, but I'm not stupid.

Before I continue, let me explain what I mean by 'monster'. Interest in these so-called 'lizard people' has been circulating for decades. Various theories and explanations have been discussed on several platforms. Although their claims are not based on provable facts – none that I'm aware of – they're not entirely wrong. 'Lizard People' is a blanket term. I don't like it, but I have to accept it. At least I'm not alone in my suspicions. Many people see them. Unfortunately, and to the peril of the planet, the phenomenon goes way deeper.

These monsters are bloodthirsty, heartless creatures, lurking in shadows, feeding off the fear of humans. They come in many shapes and sizes: from government officials, business owners, grade school teachers, you name it; some are janitors, garbage collectors and homeless people.

Some people claim that the world is run by a Satanic cult, planning some Big Event that will turn our world into a Prison Planet. I'm not claiming that either. That's beyond my scope of comprehension. I have no skin in the game. I've avoided politics and religion my entire life, and I don't like sports. At this point in my life, I'd be happy settling down with a wife, raise a family, and retire on a nice plot of land. Ugh, am I getting old, or what?

Anyway, monsters, aka Lizard People, do exist. They always have. And not just in this world. There are others worlds. Worlds where monsters don't hide; worlds where your darkest days are celebrated; where the unholy feast on the flesh of small children, bathing in their blood.

Here's another fun fact: These monsters are actual beings, like you and I. They have mothers and fathers, siblings and partners. But they're not of this Earth. Not of this dimension, in fact. Their lives are much longer than humans, and they have powers, giving them a hefty advantage over us. Have I mentioned that they're coming for your children? Okay, so why am I telling you this? Like I said, I got a call from these lofty fat cats in DC. They offered me more money than I know what to do with, and they paid upfront. Thus, after weeks of screening, testing, profiling and indoctrination, I was led into a dingy room, smelling of mouldy bread, surrounded by unsmiling faces dressed in black.

They told me things.

Let's get one thing straight: I don't trust these people. Not on my life. Nor should you. Many of them are monsters. Like I said, monsters hide in plain sight. But for whatever reason, I see them for who – or what – they truly are.

I got straight to work. As I suspected, their files were in total disarray. How anyone could let their computers become so bogged down is beyond me. Yet sadly, I've seen worse. Plenty worse. After a month or so, I was finished. Then I tackled the laptop. Yikes. Curiosity got the best of me. I did something unethical: I copied their 'Top Secret' files, easily bypassing their security. Please note: Although most IT people do this (if you've ever hired one chances are they know your dirty secrets), I've only ever done it once before, on my girlfriend's computer, and all I found was a backlog of Disney classics and Taylor Swift rarities.

The laptop holds top secret files that can get me arrested or even killed: Videos of government doctors and agents in white lab coats doing ungodly experiments on pregnant women. Many of the doctors were monsters, but not all. I suspect the human doctors are unaware of the creatures they're collaborating with.

After many sleepless nights glued to my screen, watching these experiments, I've concluded this: the monsters are breeding. They're kidnapping pregnant woman and injecting the fetuses with monster DNA. Then they erase the mother's memory. The mother goes home, remembers nothing, and gives birth to a baby monster.

There's more: Three nights ago, I discovered a monster database: their dates-of-birth, addresses, occupations and politics. This means, the secret service is aware of monsters, and has been harvesting and monitoring them. What I've learned is horrific. Once a monster is born, its offspring is also a monster. It all dates back to March 6, 1964. Soon, there'll be more of them than us.

gotta go!!! They're at my back door

OK Im back.

Its been awhile.

Busy. Busy. Yeah, starting to wish I hadn't done what i done. should never have peaked Some things are best knot knowing. Like some people should never be trusted. Especially, monsters. i hate monsters…

Better yet, i should no taken the job, although its starting to look like i had no choice, these 'people' meen business.

….

ok i'm getting 'for-real' scared now… bad vibes everywhere

they r watching me! reflection in my screen: a cold blanc stare that could chill a block of ice

something in me changing… must resissst

….

Okay, i feeling better, phew

Something is wrong. My fingers are webbed. Tongue feels thick, heavy.

My abilt8u to typer getting bad. I dunno y. ill be back tmrow to conclude miy work

….

Not much time! I'm fighting this. Bastards. Monsters everywheyre They no

ok

so im bak and soethtoii is rong. relly relly rong

i can c my reflection now. Im a monster!!

im infected

im 1 of THEM

oh no no no no no

helpf - they r watching u

save yerslf!

The Giving Tree

I was walking home from school. Autumn was blooming; the leaves were starting to change and the days were growing shorter. I took the winding path along the escarpment, which overlooks the city, because the view is staggering at that time of year. The trail mostly used by joggers and people out walking their dogs. The route is attached to a much larger trail that runs throughout the entire city and province.

I came around a bend and saw an old man sitting on the park bench between two maple trees. The bench overlooks the city skyline, and provides a gorgeous view, so it wasn't uncommon to see someone sitting there, relaxing and enjoying the generous backdrop. It's a nice spot. Because the bench faces the escarpment and not the pathway, I didn't get a good look at him, although I remember he was wearing a brown corduroy suit, brown fedora, and reading a green paperback. I passed him without a glance and was home safe and sound twenty minutes later.

A couple weeks later, as the leaves began to turn a deeper hue and the temperature slowly plummeted, I saw him there again. He was wearing the same simple suit and matching fedora. Also, he was reading that same beat-to-death green paperback. I still didn't get a good look at his face, seeing how his back was to me, but I thought nothing of it. I kept walking, and was home in a jiffy.

None of this seemed out of the ordinary. At that time, I was very much preoccupied with Ashley McGregor, and wondering whether or not she liked me the same way I liked her. It wasn't until the following spring, when the snow had melted and the green was returning to the grass and the leaves revisiting their respective trees that I spotted the old man again. Although I didn't see his face, I noticed he was wearing that brown suit and fedora, reading that same green paperback. As weeks passed, I saw him sitting on that bench more frequently: same spot, same time of day, same clothes and paperback. I began to speculate. He must be a widow, I figured, longing for the days of his youth; or maybe he was a criminal, lamenting his dark and dodgy past. My imagination was boundless. If only I could get a better look at him.

So why don't I? That question popped into my head during my final day of high school. It's a public park and he doesn't own it. So why not? If I walk past him on the bench, and head over to the edge of the bluff, as I've done countless times, I could get a better look at him. Maybe I'll snap some nice pics while I'm at it. With a panorama shot, you can capture a stunning view of the city, starting with the forest-laden West End, past the urban sprawls and trendy cafes of the downtown core, then across the industrial East End with the smokestacks and heavy smog massaging Lake Ontario. On a clear day you can even see the CN Tower peering from across the Great Lake, Ontario.

So, I did it.

I remember feeling anxious, like my heart was trying to escape from my chest; also, my palms were sweaty and my legs were packed with pins and needles. Why was I so nervous? Maybe I was afraid of confronting the severity of old age; seeing his tired, wrinkled hands and long, furrowed face, his brittle bones and sagging skin wilting beneath his simple suit. Or maybe I was just spooked. With my backpack slung over my shoulder and smartphone in my left hand, I trudged along the trail leading to the bench overlooking the city. The wind was ferocious; I relished in the shelter this small neck of woods provided. I came around the bend, and for a moment I thought the bench was empty. My heart sank. Just my luck, I thought. Then, as I came closer, the old man suddenly appeared, sitting on the bench, straight as an arrow, eyes buried in his book. He wore the same brown suit and hat.

Without propitiousness, I traversed the crunchy grass and fallen branches until I was parallel to the bench. I'd never been this close to him before. I caught a whiff of Old Spice, and was reminded of my grandfather, who passed away when I was young. My grandfather also wore a fedora hat, I recalled. I hadn't thought of him in many years. He was my father's father, and since I lived with my mother, the subject of Granddad never came up. I stole a sideways glance. He never once looked up. He simply sat on the bench staring serenely into his green paperback, well-postured and still as a morning pond, oblivious to my presence. Shaking like a leaf, I forced myself to continue. Finally, as my nerves were coming unglued and I was on the brink of a full-fledged anxiety attack, I made it to the edge of the escarpment, near the bench where he sat. I sighed, and with my camera pointed over the cliff, I captured a stunning image of a red-tailed hawk circling high above the trees. If nothing else, this pic will have made this trip worthwhile. It was straight fire, as Ashley McGregor liked to say.

Before putting my phone away, I turned and pointed the camera at the old man, snapping a pic; then I stuffed my device into my back pocket and scampered toward the beaten path. I should talk to him, I remember thinking, that would be the neighbourly thing to do. Except, now that I could see him better, I no longer wanted to talk to him. In fact, I wanted to be nowhere near the man. Something about him was creeping me out, but I couldn't put my finger on it. Although he was facing me, I couldn't make out any of his features. He was blurred, unfocused, like a mirage. I blamed it on the shadows of the trees he was sitting under, but still. Something about him seemed wrong. I don't know how else to describe it. I booted it past the old man sitting on the bench and hurried home. I ate a quick dinner, played Minecraft, then spent the night texting Ashley McGregor. (Turns out she does like me the way I like her) I brushed my teeth and went to bed and that was that. Good riddance to bad rubbish.

For the duration of that summer, I avoided the pathway along the escarpment where the old man would sit. Instead, I spent most of my time visiting my father. It was nice seeing him again. One night, as the summer was winding down and my first year of college was fast approaching, we watched baseball, and he let me drink a couple beers with him, which he'd never done before. What a guy. After the alcohol instilled its liquid courage, I asked him about my grandfather. My father looked pleasantly surprised.

"I've been thinking about him lately," he said. He went fishing through his closet and produced a dust-drenched photo album. It was big and bulky and bowling alley-blue. "Here's a blast from the past." Seeing that photo album conjured many conflicting feelings. Sometimes, I forget that there was a world before I was born, before smartphones, before the Internet...

"My father," he said, "your grandfather, was a bona fide war hero. He stormed the beaches of Normandy, and lived to tell about it. Although he rarely, if ever, would." My father was getting more choked-up with each word he spoke. Maybe it was the beer, maybe it was the biological human need to connect with his son; maybe his memories were clinging to dear life, refusing to let go. "You know," he said, after taking a good long pull from his bottle of Bud. "He was the ripe age of 47 by the time I came along. He was pushing 80 when you were born. The stubborn old mule wouldn't die," he said jokingly, then took another swig from his bottle. "He was tough as nails, I tell ya."

My father had a row of old photographs displayed neatly along the coffee table. "This is him before I was born. Way before I was born, in fact. This would've been just after the war. He must've been around 24. Jesus. Look at all those medals." The black and white photograph was in near-mint condition. It showed my grandfather clean-shaven, tall and proud, clad in his Army uniform, decorated with medals, posing in front of a single-seat fighter-bomber. "I've still got those medals. Wanna see them?"

"Yes!"

A striking smile sprouted on my father's face, which brought me joy. It was obvious how much he revelled in our time together. He was getting older and seemingly less happy with each passing day, and anytime I can cheer him up is good. He left, fetched us both another beer, then came back with a cardboard box filled with miscellaneous artifacts. "I really should do something with this junk," he said, more to himself. He pried the box open and cool-looking stuff spilled out, including Grandad's old metals. I marvelled at their aesthetics and sheer weightiness.

"This here is my parent's wedding picture," he said. "They truly loved each other. I'm sure they made everyone around them feel special." He removed the picture from the album and handed it to me. I was stunned. I'd forgotten how beautiful my grandmother was. She was so young and animated, full of hopes and dreams on her wedding day; her beauty was exemplary, her dress elegant and plush. I'd never known my grandmother; sadly, she died giving birth to my father. This is a subject that rarely gets spoken of. As my father continued sifting through these time-worn treasures, a steady stream of tears escaped the corners of his eyes.

He passed me the box of junk; I began flipping through photographs and random relics until I saw something that stopped me dead in my tracks. My blood chilled. Worse, my stomach was threatening to regurgitate all the beer and nachos I'd consumed.

"Wh-what's that?" I asked in a shaky voice.

"Huh, oh that? That was your father's favourite book. He would read it to your grandmother while she was pregnant with me. She liked that. As a child, your grandfather would often read this book to me, and whenever he did, he would go into great detail describing your grandmother." He wiped his eyes.

I stared at the green paperback with horror. Suddenly, I felt like I was a character in somebody else's story, and nothing was in my control. My father, on the other hand, was regarding the book with awe. When he tried handing it to me, I leapt off the couch in sheer panic. My father laughed and told me I was cut off. Reluctantly, and with a mind full of fear, I read the title of the paperback: The Giving Tree.

"B-but, it's a children's book."

"Yes it is. Your grandmother wanted my dad to read this to her unborn baby. She was a smart lady."

"Why did he read it to her though? Couldn't she just have read it herself?" The beer was loosening my lips, it seemed. I hated myself for asking these questions.

"That's how it was with them. Besides, my father was a wonderful speaker. He did a lot of theatre work, you know."

My father went silent. Then added, "Well, he stopped when I was born and my mother—" He paused to wipe his cheek. "—But enough talk about my parents," he said. "Let's get back to watching baseball, shall we?"

It was getting late and I told him I was ready to head home. I started gathering my belongings. It was painfully clear how sad my father was to see me go. This is why I didn't like going there, it always ended in sorrow. It's not his fault, I reminded myself as I put on my sneakers, it would be the same if I lived here and was forced to visit my mother on weekends and holidays. Leaving one parent to visit the other is never easy.

Just before my Uber arrived, my father showed me one last picture of my grandfather. "This is the last picture I have of him," he said, wistfully. I regarded the picture with gut-wrenching misery. Yet, there was truth inside this time-worn photograph, no matter how much it hurt. In it, my grandfather was wearing a brown corduroy suit and fedora; he was sitting on a modest kitchen table staring directly at the camera. He looked terribly fatigued, his face hard and chiselled from the ravages of time. Next to him, lay a small, green paperback: The Giving Tree. I nearly fainted. This was the same old man I'd seen sitting at the park bench. This came as quite a shock, as you can imagine.

Then I remembered the picture I'd snapped of him at the escarpment the last time I'd seen him. I'd forgotten about it. Timorously, I reached for my phone, being sure not to raise suspicion from my father, and scrolled through my pics until I found what I was looking for. The picture was clear as day. In it, the old man's brilliant blue eyes seemed to jump out at me, the small green paperback clenched in his hands was clearly visible: The Giving Tree. I compared the two photographs. There was no doubt that these were both the same men. But how?

Before leaving, my father surprised me with a question. He wanted to know if I'd like to take my grandfather's medals home with me; pass them down to the next generation and all. I accepted, but only if I could also take the small, green paperback as well. He seemed unfazed by this. Probably, it was the beer.

We awkwardly embraced, then we said our goodbyes. When I left, I carried with me a new sense of purpose. I felt I'd grown up considerably that summer, and was ready to face the world and its many challenges. Moreover, I'd rejuvenated my bond with my father, something I'd wanted to do for many years. Now it was time to do the same with my grandfather.

That's where I saw my first ghost. I'll be sure to visit the bench edging the escarpment this afternoon, as I've done many times since starting college. I can honestly say that I've enjoyed each visit with my grandfather, who continues to sit alone on the park bench overlooking the city. Maybe today he can read to me. Yes, that would be nice. Or better yet, maybe I'll read to him. I would like that. I'll start with The Giving Tree.

My Band Opened For MURDER - They Killed It

MURDER assassinated the entire audience at the stroke of midnight. Everyone except me. I was the only survivor. Sex and drugs saved my life.

If you're into death metal music, then you're probably a fan of MURDER. Hailing from Scandinavia, their following is ridiculous. How Ricky, the manager of Dive Bar, (that's actually the bar's name), managed to book them is beyond me. But he did. And he's dead because of it.

Toronto was in full lockdown. It was getting ridiculous, to be honest. I'd been out of work for nearly a year, same as my boss Ricky. So when I got the call from him a week before Christmas, it came as a surprise.

"Brandon, my man, whatcha been up to?" He didn't wait for an answer. "Good. Good. Now listen, I didn't want to text you this and have you screw it up, so I called instead. Hope that's alright." Same old Ricky. "I need your band to play a secret staff Christmas party at the Dive Bar. You'll be performing in the basement. That way no one will hear or see anything. You good?"

This time he waited for a reply.

"Um, yes. I'll have to check with the band, but yeah."

I checked. The band was excited to play. My band is called SSIK. This was our first gig in nine months. We had an absolute blast, plugging in and cranking out tunes. After the show, Ricky pulled me into his smoky little office and asked if SSIK was interested in playing a private party for NYE, opening for MURDER.

"MURDER? Hell yeah."

What could possibly go wrong?

MURDER brought a guillotine. It was the coolest thing I've ever seen in my life. It was silver and sharp, and dare I say, sexy, in a medieval torture kind of way. They also brought a thirteen-person road crew who took twelve hours setting up for the show. The band and their crew refused to speak to anyone, and when they did, they spoke Scandinavian, so no one understood what they were saying. It didn't matter. They were MURDER.

A hundred lucky patrons squeezed into the Dive Bar basement that night. It was a killer show, to say the least.

SSIK's set went off without a hitch. I sang, um well, screamed, better than I've ever screamed in my entire life. We even did an encore, and crushed it. Then came MURDER.

Typically, when a band uses a fog machine, they don't poison the crowd with the stuff, but MURDER did. They emptied three full canisters as they hit the stage. One woman, dressed in a black crushed-velvet dress, dropped dead. She was sitting on the leather couch in the corner, clutching her asthma puffer; nobody noticed her until the cops came, an hour and a half later. By then the Dive Bar looked like a scene from the goriest horror movie ever made. I'll let you pick which one.

MURDER wore black leather gear; they had long greasy hair and faces painted like demons. I was impressed. Their singer had metal studs pierced over his entire body and a bloody pentagram stitched onto his bare chest. They opened their set with their most popular song, Crusted Corpse. During the guitar solo, a roadie handed the singer a large Samurai sword. The audience wowed.

The drummer kicked into the second song. The singer, brandishing the colossal silver sword, pulled some dude on stage. Everyone cheered. The dude started headbanging, clearly enjoying himself, oblivious to his gruesome fate. During what may have been the chorus of the song, the singer swung the sword and cut the dude's head off. The head rolled along the stage and lodged in between the monitors. The guitarist kicked the head to the side of the stage like it was nothing. The crowd erupted. Amazing special effects! Woot!

Except it wasn't special effects. It was real. I was standing on the side of the stage and watched as the dead dude's head rolled clumsily to my feet. Blood and brains and bone spewed everywhere. It was revolting. Stupidly, (remember: it was NYE, I'd just performed and I was getting paid in alcohol, so I was extremely drunk), I punted the severed head into the audience, who proceeded to knock it around like a beach ball.

The singer kept shouting orders at the crowd; the crowd clung to his every word. The crowd was bloodthirsty, stark raving mad. I had a sobering moment, realising just how depraved these people had become. With so much pent-up stress being released all at once, these people were out of their minds. Everyone wanted to be rid of 2020 as quickly as possible. And I didn't blame them. If they only knew what MURDER was planning for them.

I searched for Ricky, who was behind the bar serving drinks. The lineup to the bar was ridiculous. I convinced myself nothing was wrong. MURDER, following in the tradition of Alice Cooper, GWAR and Slipknot, were merely putting on an elaborate show with plenty of shock value. It was all part of the show. Fun for the whole family.

Then came the guillotine.

The singer requested a volunteer. A sexy middle-aged woman (dare I say MILF?) jumped on stage. She had wild frizzy red hair, a tight black dress and Doc Martin boots. I knew this woman. Her name was Brenda.

At once, the singer slapped her, gagged her, tied her arms with rope and shoved her head under the blade. The crowd was murderous, chanting OFF WITH HER HEAD; OFF WITH HER HEAD... All eyes remained on the guillotine. The drummer started a long, speedy drum roll; first quiet, then louder and louder. The bassist started an evil-sounding groove. The guitarist joined in. It was the most horrible song I've ever heard. The music got louder and louder, rising into a frenzy then WACK! Down came the blade.

Brenda's decapitated head fell to the front of the stage; her lifeless body twitched then went still. The singer jumped off the speaker, picked up her severed head, and waved it high as though it were his trophy. Then he chucked it into the crowd. I guess two heads are better than one.

While Brenda's ghastly head was quickly being pulverised, her lifeless blues eyes remained open. Apparently, she wanted to watch the remainder of the show.

Still, no one flinched. I sensed this wasn't an act, but I was too drunk to do anything about it. Plus, I was in shock. It's not everyday you see two people get their heads cut off. I just wanted to leave.

MURDER carried on with the show. Their volume was deafening. Nervously, I checked the time: it was almost midnight. The bassist, who looked like Gene Simmons but somehow uglier, crept closer and closer to the crowd. His bass was shaped like a battle axe. This singer pulled another guy on stage and tossed him toward the bassist, who, unless my eyes deceived me, used his bass to slice the man's stomach open. Blood and guts spilled out all over the sticky stage. Even over the incredible noise, I heard that man's final scream. His dead hands were making the devil horns sign. It was like a scene from Metalocalypse. I felt like I was tripping on bad LSD.

The singer reached into the dead man's intestines and pulled out a handful of stringy red goop. By this time, people were rushing onto the stage like savages. The singer smeared guts all over some teenage girl's face. She licked her face, lapping it up; her teeth turning cherry-red. The delight on the singer's face was undeniable.

The band carried on. Now it was the guitarist's turn. He took his patch cord and used it to strangle an audience member, wrapping the long black cord around some guy's neck until it snapped. I watched in horror as his eyes bulged out of his head; his face turned bright red, then blue, then a ghostly white. The guitarist tossed the fresh corpse off the stage back into the crowd, who then ripped the body to shreds, all without missing a note.

By now, people were beginning to panic, but only a precious few. The drummer started slinging his drum sticks into the crowd like spears. There must've been razor blades shoved in them, because I saw a drum stick sticking out of some cute college girl's eye. She freaked out; and using both hands, she pried the stick out of her head, removing her eyeball in the process. The girl next to her snatched the eyeball and took a bite. It must've tasted awful because she immediately spat it out.

Terrified and confused, I escaped to the restroom, only to discover two gorgeous Goth chicks doing lines off each other's breasts in the washroom stall. This was certainly the best part of the evening. They giggled; then the Goth chicks showed me a helluva good time, before retreating to the front of the stage, just in time for MURDER's grand finale.

The smell of the stall was inexcusable. Still I waited in the urine–soaked stall, deciding my next move. The coke sobered me up enough to call 911. But I was too late. I heard the screaming. I knew this was it: the countdown to 2021.

The band stopped playing at 11:59. The singer, standing at the front of the stage, pulled out his iPhone and started going live. The audience went berserk. Using broken English, he began the countdown.

10!

9!

8!

7!

6!

5!

4!

3!

2!

1!

HAPPY NEW YEAR!!!

I stayed hidden in the stall, listening to the machine gun frenzy: *POP POP POP POP POP*. The sound of one hundred people being executed. MURDER's road crew had blocked off all the exits. The audience was trapped. After a minute of non-stop machine gun fire, the doomed audience was dead. The singer then turned the gun onto his bandmates and crew, then finally, himself. Everyone died but me.

I did another bump in the stinky stall and laughed, despite myself. Wouldn't ya know it? Sex and drugs just saved my life.

The Scarecrow

Growing up, my best friend was Robert Moretti, a fast-talking Italian boy who was bigger and tougher than most kids our age. I'd known him since we were preschoolers. Just beyond Robert's house was a dead-end street. One of the houses on it was the Hanson house, a supposed haunted house, which inspired countless urban legends and ghoulish tales. Back then, the creepy house was occupied by a mother and son. The mother was said to be a witch. The boy, Tommy Hansen, was close to our age, but nobody played with him or anything. In fact, he was rarely seen leaving his house. He must've been home-schooled or something.

One particular Halloween, Robert devised the brilliant plan of trick-or-treating at the haunted house, which we did, and I damn-near got scared to death.

It was 1990; Teenage Mutant Ninja Turtles was all the rage, so Robert and I dressed up as Michelangelo and Leonardo respectively. Oh, to be twelve again. With our bags stuffed with candy, we slowly worked our way towards the old Hansen house. When we came to the house, we stopped and regarded it for a moment. The house was big and ugly and made of stone. Plus, it smelled of worms.

The moon was nearly full, the air was cool and crisp. A smattering of trick-or-treaters were huddled outside the Hansen house, but not many, and they didn't stay long. "Hurry up, Paul," Robert said, nervously. I walked tepidly along the pathway running beside the driveway which led to the front door. A scarecrow was sitting lifelessly on a wooden bench. It looked kinda scary, with its overalls stuffed with hay and filthy scarf; on its head was a spine-chilling jack-o'-lantern with slanted eyes and a toothy grin that made me cringe. It looked like it wanted to bite me. I could feel its empty eyes penetrating me as I got nearer. By this time, it was just me and Robert, all the other trick-or-treaters had disappeared.

Robert nudged me onward. Grudgingly, I lumbered on, ignoring that hideous Halloween prop seated on the bench, until I finally reached the front door to the Hansen house. I was nervous, but I wouldn't let it show. With Robert by my side, egging me on, I pushed the glowing red doorbell. The house howled. Then, while preparing to come face to face with the Hansen Witch, the scarecrow lunged at me, arms extended, yanking my neck.

I screamed, dropped my bag of candy and split. Robert followed, laughing like a loon. We booked it down the walkway, away from the Hansen house, and never looked back. I went home scared and sad and candyless. It was my worst Halloween ever.

Robert teased me for a month about how scared I was, later confessing that the lunging scarecrow was an annual prank the Hansens played on the public. The scarecrow was in fact Tommy. A great costume, I agreed. But I wanted revenge. That's why the following year, when Robert suggested we use a video camera to record other kids getting scared to death, then send the tape to America's Funniest Home Videos with Bob Saget, I happily agreed.

I borrowed my father's camera. Back then, those cameras were highly regarded and quite expensive; so, when I say borrowed, I use that term loosely.

The sky was ominous and dull; the streetlights mingled with the pale moonlight creating the perfect backdrop for our childish prank. Robert dressed up as the Terminator, I was Axl Rose. We crept towards the Hansen house. A handful of parents could be seen loitering on the sidewalk, but only a few.

When we arrived at the Hansen house, a group of kids wearing silly costumes approached the front door. Catwoman pressed the doorbell. When the door opened, the little girl shouted Trick or Treat! I could see the sneer in Mrs. Hansen's face as she gave away her toothsome treats. She gave me chills. Her costume was elaborate, flawless. Her skin was sickly green and covered in warts; her long and pointed nose was as sharp as her devilish smirk; her teetering black hat sparkled under the glow of the waning porch light. She really was a witch, and I refused to get any closer to her.

"Gimme your camera," Robert demanded. He grabbed the camera. "There he is!" He pointed to the scarecrow on the bench. "Look at Tommy in that ridiculous costume." Robert was doing his best to sound brave, but I knew better.

Sitting solemnly on the brown bench was the scarecrow with the pumpkin head. Same as before. Only this year it seemed uglier. Its crudely carved eyes regarded me with disdain, its dagger-like teeth daring me to come closer. I knew it was Tommy, but you wouldn't know it from looking at the thing.

Robert pointed the camera, then told me to get going. Inspecting every golden maple leaf that crunched under my boots, I left the safety of the sidewalk and trudged toward the Hansen house.

"Hurry up, fool!" Robert insisted, shoving me forward.

I tried to hurry but my feet were not cooperating. In truth, I was spooked, both of the scarecrow, and of the witch waiting at the front door. Finally, I found my courage. What was I afraid of? I'm thirteen years old: I'm too old to be spooked. As I got going, my eyes never left the scarecrow. Any minute now, Tommy will leap out from the bench and terrify that unsuspecting little girl. He didn't. Instead, after Cat Woman and her friends collected their candy, they said thank-you and then scurried off. The scarecrow did not budge.

Another group of trick-or-treaters arrived. We let them go ahead of us. This was our chance. The kids passed the bench and collected their candy. The scarecrow was unresponsive to the fresh batch of trick-or-treaters. They came and went, disappearing into the dark of night.

Anger was stirring inside me. 365 days of pent-up teenage angst was about to burst. With unwarranted bravery, I charged at the scarecrow on the bench. Robert shouted, "Wait!" but it was too late. Unfortunately, I tripped on my shoelaces (a lifelong habit) and fell flat on my face, directly in front of the scarecrow. Its soiled, black boots were too big for any boy my age. When I looked up, directly into its pumpkin-carved eyes, I cringed. In them, I saw a flickering candle flame, blowing in the breeze.

Robert, still pointing the camera, shouted, "Trick-or-treat, you stupid pumpkin brain!" and started laughing and jumping up and down. Mrs. Hanson spat and cursed. The cackling of her voice sent chills down my spine. When I looked back at the scarecrow, Tommy's grey eyes appeared suddenly. He winked, then he lumbered towards me.

"AAAAAHHHH!"

By now the other trick-or-treaters were laughing and pointing and asking Tommy Hanson to show them the inside of his pumpkin head. Tommy refused. Instead, he simply sat back down on the bench and went still, waiting for his next unsuspecting victim.

I was furious. And deeply embarrassed, which made it worse. Robert dragged me away from the front door. He was spooked by the Hanson Witch, but he'd never admit to it. We teased each other, then went home. For the second year in a row, I cleaned the poop-stained from my underpants.

The next day at school we shared a heartfelt laugh. Robert, who refused to return my father's camera, eventually gave it back (after we'd watched the footage over and over again at his place). The funniest part, of course, was my reaction. One moment the scarecrow was sitting languidly on the bench, the next moment it was attacking me. Har-dee-har-har.

We soon forgot about this incident, seeing how there was other cool stuff happening at school that stole our interest; and needless to say, I never bothered sending the tape to America's Funniest Home Videos. Eventually, the video camera, along with the tape, ended up in a taped-up cardboard box, waiting in my father's garage for thirty years. When he passed away this summer, my son Brandon discovered it. Brandon, who is now the same age as I was on that tape, was intrigued by this relic from the past. He's an audio geek, and currently going through his analogue infatuation stage.

Brandon took the tape, digitized it, then played it for me. It was a blast from the past, let me tell you. I thought it was hysterical; Brandon, on the other hand, was alarmed.

"Watch what happens when we zoom in," he said, in a shaky voice.

When he zoomed in, I shuttered. This must be a mistake. He assured me it was not. He backtracked and I watched the scene again, this time with a careful eye.

There I was at thirteen, dressed as my favourite rock star, standing six feet in front of the scarecrow on the bench.

"Now, watch this," Brandon said.

My stomach was in knots. I watched that young boy on the screen, who looks eerily like Brandon, only smaller, come alive. The camera showed my back, as I charged the bench, falling flat on my face. The camera shakes as Robert shouts something, but only for a moment, then he zooms in on the scarecrow. Without warning, the scarecrow springs out of his sitting position, arms stretched out, and attacks me. I scream and trip and fall down again. I'd forgotten that part. That must've been when I crapped my pants.

At once, we're ambushed by a bunch of bratty boys, who swarm the scarecrow, asking questions, then the video cuts off.

Brandon tweaked the settings on the screen and rewound the video. "Now check this out." He pressed play. Only now, it played in slow motion, zoomed in entirely on the scarecrow.

"Just as I suspected," I said nervously under my breath. "Well, I'll be."

"Dad," Brandon said, "What the hell is that thing?"

I could see clearly inside the jack-o'-lantern; and yes, there was a small flame flickering inside it. Except it wasn't an actual flame, probably a cheap Dollar Store replica. But still.

"Now, here's where it gets extra creepy," he said. "Watch carefully." He pointed to the screen.

I watched. For a moment the scarecrow seems unaffected, lifeless. Then suddenly a face appears inside the pumpkin head. "What the…" I muttered.

"Right?"

"Play it again."

He did.

I gasped.

"That's impossible," Brandon said.

He was intrigued, although the fear in his eyes was beyond doubt. But there was something else in his eyes: The inevitable curiosity of a thirteen-year-old boy. It wasn't long before he'd convinced me to bring him and his best friend Bruno Moretti to that spooky old house for Halloween. Apparently, Bruno knew all about the Hanson house.

I drove by the Hanson house this morning to scope it out. I hadn't been to that part of town in years. What amazed me as I drove past the place was how unaffected by time the house seemed. To be fair, the place is over 150 years-old, so what's another thirty years, right? Still. I didn't like it.

Nor did I like the scarecrow sitting corpse-like on the bench out on the veranda. I pulled the car over and got out. I'm not crazy, I told myself, as I trotted toward the scarecrow, smart phone in hand. Just being safe.

I pointed my phone at the scarecrow and pressed record. I stood for a moment, six feet in front of it, unsure of what to do next. I waved goodbye jokingly, then I got back inside my car and tore out of there. My heart was beating faster than I care to admit.

I didn't tell Brandon about my venture, but I wish I had. Because there's no way in hell that I was taking him trick-or-treating at the Hansen house. No matter how much of a fuss he makes.

I just watched the video and saw something disturbing. When I zoomed in (even an old fart like me can do that on my Android), the Hanson Witch was hovering by the front door, leering at me; although I swear, she wasn't there at the time.

That's not all. The scarecrow, who was sitting listlessly on the brown bench by the front door, bolted upright. The flickering candle flame inside the jack-o'-lantern switched to a boy's eye. It winked at me. Then it lunged.

I'd forgotten that part.

Help! A Zombie Apocalypse Is Upon Us

I've just learned a terrible truth: Our world is under attack. By zombies. Let me start at the beginning:

Gramps served in WW2. He was eighteen when he enlisted. Gramps rarely spoke of the war. In fact, I know very little about the man. Until recently. The other day, I received an anonymous package. Inside the package was a dusty, old tape player and cassette. I was shocked. I hadn't seen a tape deck in years. Then I pressed play.

Gramps's voice was ravaged by old age. Tears trickled down my face as he spoke. But soon, I was petrified. If what he said is true, then the world is in BIG trouble. With much care, I've transcribed, word for word, what he said. (Please forgive the crudeness of Gramp's speech. He's extremely old, and he comes from a different era.)

"Nathan, if you're hearing this, then I'm probably dead. Dead, or dying. Either way, I hope you hear me well. I won't be going into how this tape came into your possession. So don't bother asking. In time, you will receive another package. Then you will have no choice but to believe what I'm about to tell you."

(Random movements, chair squeaking).

"You'll have to bear with me."

(Coughing).

"Do you ever get the sense that someone is in the room with you, even when you're alone? Do you hear your name whispered from nowhere? Or feel that someone, or something, is hovering above your bed while you sleep?

"The answer is probably yes, although your mind may trick itself into saying 'no'. You're an adult now. Adults are dull. They lose their sixth sense. Not me. How could I? You see, when I was in the army, a million years ago it would seem, I was captured by the Nazis. Ugh. Rotten bastards."

(Papers ruffling).

"I was nineteen. The other prisoners were near-death when I arrived. Our cell was filthy beyond description, with rats as big as German tanks, scurrying across the cold, damp floor. Hmph. Those rats were treated with more dignity than we were. Mostly, I remember the smell. Rotten flesh, feces, sweat and decay. Ugh. Months went by. I was certain to die there. And I almost did. Oh, the horror of it all. But I'll spare you the gory details."

(Inaudible).

"Okay, so let's get to the point, shall we? This isn't a war story, after all. Unbeknownst to me, the war was ending. The Americans came to the rescue. About time, I may add. Suddenly, the Nazis were nervous. One day, a large wooden crate was dropped into the cell. By now, the other prisoners were dead. It was only me. I...I won't tell you what I did to survive."

(Long pause).

"Sometime in the middle of the night, I opened the crate. Took every ounce of strength, it did. I knew this would land me in a whole heap of trouble. But what did I care? Besides, this gave me something to do.

"Inside the crate were paintings. Magnificent treasures. Against my better judgement, I placed some paintings around the cell. Bold, I was. Then I slept. Sometime in the wee hours of the night, I heard a voice:

" 'Chester,' the voice whispered. 'Psst. Chester!' "

"It kept repeating my name. Half asleep and sick with malnutrition, I grumbled, telling the guard to eat a turd.

"Then it poked me. I froze. Someone was lying next to me, cold as a corpse, breathing down my neck. I sat upright, soaring with adrenaline. My hands were clenched, ready to strangle the Nazi scumbag.

"To my amazement, the cell was empty. Save for the corpses of course, which were buzzing with flies and maggots, and stinking worse than a plague of sewer rats. I shook my weary head, cursing my stupidity, then sucked the sweat from my fingers before returning to sleep. Oh, how horrible those days were."

(Coughing).

"The voice returned. Then I saw it."

(Long pause).

"It…it came through the painting. I swear on God's good grace it did. It was ugly. Repulsive. Like a hideous monster drawn by a child. Its body was simple and small, but its head was huge, with droopy eyes as wide as fighter planes. Its gaping mouth exposed a pallet of pointed teeth, and a tongue that could smack the smirk right off your face.

"Chester,' it said grimly, raising the hair on my arms.

"Finally, I found my breath. I was petrified. Not only was a zombie haunting me…um, that's what they are…more about that later…I didn't want the guards to hear me. Turns out, they'd split. But how the hell was I to know? I didn't get the memo. When I responded, my voice was thin and weak, and barely recognizable:

" 'Whatcha want?'

"Then the most amazing thing happened: The creature flew from the painting and landed on my chest. It made terrible grunting noises, like a dog in heat. When it's wart-infested tongue touched my chin, I yelped. But the damned thing wouldn't let up. It didn't take too long before I realised what it was doing: Feeding.

"Anger arrived like a cavalry. I went on a warpath. To my surprise, the creature recoiled. It scurried inside the painting, but continued to stare at me with its all-knowing eyes and disfigured face.

"My mind and body went numb. I must've passed out. When I woke up, the damned thing was chomping on me again. Its teeth like tiny razors, stabbing my infected body, as it sucked the life from my soul.

"I…I don't remember much after that. Fortunately, within the coming days or weeks, I was rescued. You can imagine the relief. After spending months in a hospital, I was brought home. The war was over. The fighting finally ceased.

"I found work at a printing shop. It was decent work and it paid the bills. Soon thereafter, I met Helen, your grandmother. We married. Life was good for a while. Then sadly, our first child Michael, died very young. You can imagine the grief. Next came your father. Spry as a spring chicken.

"When your father was three or four, your grandmother started acting strange. And that's putting it mildly. She'd burst into a room full of people and start talking gibberish, making up words and senseless phrases.

"Sometimes she'd be naked, or wearing a lampshade on her head. Twice she tried setting the house on fire. Many such incidents occurred, which I won't get into. Ultimately, Helen was deemed 'insane and unfit' by the doctors, and she was institutionalised."

(Random noises, possibly weeping).

"Remember, this was a different world, Nathan. You must understand this. Shock therapy was still being administered. Ugh. Over the years, your grandmother's condition worsened. So much so, that visitors were no longer permitted, including me. I fought like hell, but it was a losing battle. Some years later, I received a letter stating she'd died of natural causes. Yeah, right. By then it was just me and your father. Oh, we fought like foes.

"One day, when I arrived home from work, there was a terrible commotion coming from his bedroom. Your father was bawling. The door was locked. Without thinking, I booted down the door. What I saw still haunts me:

"Your father was on the bed, clutching his throat. Eyes like springs popping from his young head; spittle and snot spewing from his cherry-red face. His hair was in disarray, his t-shirt soaked in sweat. His eyes scared me the most. They looked…um…non-human. In them, I saw the zombie. Somehow, the ghastly creature found me, and was possessing my boy, like it had done to my wife. Suddenly, things were adding up.

"You see, Nathan, up until then, I'd forgotten about the zombie in the painting. Now those memories were flooding my mind. It was clear: That zombie was ruining my life. Without hesitating, I pulled your father close, hearing the boy's heart beat against mine, and told the creature to go away. Or else. I snarled, hissed and moaned. It worked. The air in the room stilled. Your father calmed down. His eyes returned to normal.

"A few years later, I brought this up, seeing if he'd remembered. Your father freaked out, calling me a liar and a terrible father. Then he stormed away."

(Sniffles, plus random sounds, which could be him blowing his nose).

"After Helen left, people started talking. Rumours spread like wildfire. People accused me of abusing my wife. Blaming me for her demise. Not only that, your father was bullied mercilessly. Damn near killed the boy. Broke my heart."

(Sniffles).

"Your father never forgave me. That's why I wasn't around much. He wouldn't let me near you."

(Chair squeaking, papers ruffled).

"Life got weird. Flickering lights, appliances running themselves, strange voices in the still of night, footprints leading to the front door, then vanishing without a trace. Sometimes things would disappear. I'd put my car keys on the end table, as I did every night before bed, and they'd vanish. Same with my cigarettes. Don't get me started on the remote control! Sheesh!

"Eventually, when I could no longer take it, I confided in a pal. Big mistake. I'll spare you the details, but word got around that I was bat-shit crazy, and me and your father were driven out of town. He hated me for that.

"Eventually, I did find someone to confide in. A colleague. Cathy was her name. She believed me. Cathy was a good worker. Plus, she had no problems with old fogies like me. (Laughs). Now, don't get the wrong impression. Our friendship was purely platonic. Cathy…um…liked other women. But that's neither here nor there."

(Long pause).

"Phew…telling this is harder than I thought."

(Papers shuffling).

"Cathy was extremely clever. She developed these special glasses. With them, she saw what the naked eye could not. These glasses made zombies…or spirits, as she called them…visible. I'll never forget the first time I tried them on. My head hit the ceiling.

"Those creatures were all around us, crowding the office. Cathy's desk had one living in the grains of the wood. Mine did too. Every painting was possessed. Plus the couch, coffee table, lamp, radio…you name it. It started making sense. You see Nathan, zombies are everywhere, hiding under our very noses, and we never suspected a damn thing.

"Cathy and I would get together on Sundays, drink coffee, and discuss the meaning of all this. She'd go to nightclubs on weekends, wearing those special glasses of hers. Turns out, alcohol is a conduit for the spirit realm. Zombies…true zombies…not the brainless buggers in horror flicks who walk and talk and shoot big guns…thrive on alcohol. Alcohol gives them special power of over us. Hmph. No wonder they're called spirits.

"Zombies influence the living. Make us do evil deeds. Make us hurt one another. That's how they feed. The more misery, the better the meal.

"Now get this: after wearing Cathy's glasses for a few weeks, our eyes adjusted. Meaning, we started seeing them without the glasses. Ugh. This was something I could've done without, thank-you-very-much. Nearly ruined my life.

"Once, while I was driving home from work, I saw a horrific accident. Traffic was thick; the sun was at that spot where it blinds you. In the lane next to me was a young man singing along to the radio. He was fully immersed. Beside him was a zombie. Its claw-like hands were clutching the steering wheel. The creature snarled, then veered suddenly into oncoming traffic. BAM. So many casualties. A tragedy.

"I've seen this happen many times. Ugh. No wonder there's so many car crashes. Those bloodthirsty zombies cause the crashes. Ruthless, they are. And hungry."

(Long pause).

"To this day, I don't have an answer. Those zombies are everywhere. Even trees! Ever look at a tree and see it staring back at you? It is. Chew on that one for a while! Anyways, this was all too much for Cathy, whose heart was as big as an ocean. It ruined her. One day she quit, and I never saw her again."

(Coughing).

"I…I can't blame her. If our world is under attack…and it is…by spirits from another dimension, then what's the point? Oh, how I wish I never learned this terrible truth. But once you see them, you can't unsee them. Believe me, I've tried.

"Mass shootings became rampant. What do you think the real cause of this is? Guns? Hell no. Although they certainly speed up the process. Zombies! Like I said, they're influencers. And since they're invisible, they have free rein over us. Once they find a suitable victim…someone depressed or under the influence of drugs and alcohol…or simply in the wrong place at the wrong time…they attack.

"I've seen this so many times I've lost track. Ugh. Those creatures are the cause of almost every tragedy. And I still haven't found a way to stop them. Now, I'm old and dying."

(A woman's voice is heard, Grampa shoos her away).

"This is where you come in, Nathan. Maybe you can stop them. Or at the very least, warn others. There must be a way to stop those bastards. Otherwise…"

(Heavy coughing).

"Nathan, I'm dying. Don't worry about that. I should've been dead long ago. I'm older than dirt. Death will be a relief. But before I go, I'll let you in on a secret:

"Hospitals are Zombie Headquarters. Now get this: I've befriended one. Hot damn, I did! Goes by the name Hugo.

"Hugo told me things. First off, zombies can, in fact, eat human food. But only if it's offered to them. Problem is, who the hell would do that? They're invisible, for starters. And evil. But believe you me, they'll do anything for pie and ice cream. *Anything*. Because of this, I've made Hugo an ally. I leave him offerings every night, and he tells me things. Terrible things. The more he tells me, the more he gets fed.

"Remember this, Nathan! This could be useful. If only I'd learned this when I was your age."

(Coughing and hacking, followed by the female voice, presumably a nurse).

"I'd better hurry. Not much time left. Apparently… this is coming from Hugo's own words…zombies are waging war against humanity! We're in a spiritual war. Good versus evil.

"That's why this world is in such a wretched state. Those unholy beings are influencing the politicians. Making them do terrible deeds. But not only politicians. Anyone with influence. This is true, Nathan. But don't take my word on it. Soon, you'll see for yourself."

(Shuffling noises).

"Uh oh, the nurse is back. I must go now. Hope I said enough. And Nathan…I…I…love you boy. Always have. Be brave. And remember: They're as afraid of you, as you are…or will be…of them!"

(End of recording)

Three weeks later, a package arrived. Sure enough, inside the tightly sealed box was a pair of peculiar-looking spectacles. The left lens was normal. The right lens was deep purple, and coated with something peculiar. Needless to say, the moment I put them on my life changed. For the worse.

I couldn't believe my eyes. My place was full of them. Attached to my bedroom door was a plague of zombies. The largest (and meanest-looking) was staring at me. It had a big, bushy beard with a heavyset jaw and strict eyebrows, and was wearing what appeared to be a cowboy hat. Above it was an alien-shaped head with square eyes and licorice lips. It snarled at me.

There were others. I had to turn away. My mind couldn't handle it. In haste, I removed the glasses. But the fear remained.

Although I couldn't see them, I certainly could feel them.

How did I not notice this before? When something touched my shoulder, I nearly died.

Then I heard my name being called, although my apartment was empty.

"Nathan," the voice whispered, mockingly. "Naaaathan."

The glasses quickly returned to my face. I gasped. My gym bag was looking back at me. It too was possessed. This creature had sad, droopy eyes and a Tom Waits' style bowler hat. It hissed. I crept backwards, until my back was against the wall.

Gramps was right. They're everywhere. Clinging to furniture, stuck in the sofa, hidden in tables and chairs, attached to the TV. My tie-dye tapestry was infested. I stopped counting at twelve.

Disturbing thoughts crowded my eggshell mind, as I pretended to sleep.

The following day I got the phone call.

Gramps died.

Even as I type this, a pocket-size demon with hollowed eyes and spiked horns attached to its monstrous head, is staring back at me from my computer screen. It snarled.

I feel helpless. Not to mention scared out of my wits.

All at once, I see Gramps's conundrum. Who do I confide in? Who would believe me?

I have no answers.

So, after another sleepless night on the creature-infused couch, I've decided to write Gramps's story.

Maybe you will know what to do. Maybe you will make your own pair of glasses and see for yourself.

But don't say I never warned you:

About the Author:

Marcus Starr is the critically acclaimed author of *Nora's Curse*, his breakthrough horror novel - and now, the newly released *Monsters in the Moonlight* collection of short stories.

The author is also a musician/songwriter and private music instructor, having performed in an assortment of bands/artists and solo projects, with numerous recordings and albums. His music spans blues rock, funk rock, jam rock, country blues, fingerstyle blues and more.

Marcus Starr earned a diploma in Jazz Guitar, having completed the Applied Music Program at Mohawk College in Hamilton ON. During the pandemic he focused his creative efforts on writing a novel, while penning horror stories on Reddit under the pseudonym u/CallMeStarr.

His efforts quickly paid off. Marcus Starr became a two-time winner of the prestigious ODD & CRYPTIC Award in 2022 and 2023.

Marcus Starr is currently residing in the GTA, and is set to embark on his sophomore novel: *House of the Hungry Ghosts*. For more information regarding Marcus Starr, please visit: marcusstarrmusic.com.

www.ingramcontent.com/pod-product-compliance
Lightning Source LLC
Chambersburg PA
CBHW060414310726
48976CB00003B/1047